Bro

The Gre

# The Green Dwarf

## A Tale of the Perfect Tense

Charlotte Brontë

ET REMOTISSIMA PROPE

**100 PAGES**

100 PAGES
Published by Hesperus Press Limited
4 Rickett Street, London sw6 1ru
www.hesperuspress.com

*The Green Dwarf* first published by Hesperus Press Limited, 2003

Foreword © Libby Purves, 2003

ISBN: 1-84391-048-9

# CONTENTS

# FOREWORD

It used to be a common sneer to call a story or a person's imagination 'novelettish'. Everyone knew what it meant: melodramatic, slushy, improbable, rich in wish-fulfilment and exotic locations, but deficient in psychology, logic, and serious exploration of the human condition. The novelettes which people meant when they used the word in this way were romantic penny dreadfuls, designed to be read by gaping housemaids, idle adolescents, frustrated spinsters, or discontented wives with a short attention span. The ones which drew their romance from the Gothic-exotic stream (rather than mere aristocratic fantasy about lords and beggar-maids) found themselves mercilessly sent up by Jane Austen in *Northanger Abbey*, since which time it has barely been safe to introduce a raven, turret or monk into any work of fiction without provoking giggles.

The expression has dropped out of common use now: only a few critics would speak of a work as being 'novelettish' The descendants of these literary daydreams have multiplied and diversified, all the way from the wig-and-jabot romances of Georgette Heyer, to the headlong lustfulness of the chick-lit generation. But to remind us what the novelette could do at its rollicking peak, safe in the hands of an excitable seventeen year old destined to write one of the greatest novels of all time, here is Charlotte Brontë's *The Green Dwarf*. And it's a cracker.

It was written when, long clear of her harsh clergy boarding-school, she had spent a happier eighteen months at Roe Head school, some twenty miles from Haworth, too dutifully busy with her studies to attempt much fiction. When she began again, prompted by her brother Branwell's overblown attempts, she produced two novelettes: the

*Foundling* and *The Green Dwarf*. She borrowed Branwell's city 'Verdopolis', and bolted on all manner of preposterousness about 'The African Olympic Games', knightly figures in green lacing, withered hags in woodland castles, and lowly lovers casting off their disguise and announcing their titles in the best ballad tradition. The influence of Sir Walter Scott is somewhat heavier on her than the rules of punctuation, and were it not for the solicitude of Hesperus Press in offering some discreet commas and quotation marks, this work in the original would have more than a touch of Daisy Ashford about it:

> ' "Come with me then, Emily, shake off at once the shackles which restrain you! Free yourself from the importunities of a villain! I will take you to my mountainous lands in the north, and you shall be at once Countess of St Clair and lady of seven thousand of the bravest warriors that ever gathered round a chieftain's banner. My castle on Elimbos is larger than your uncle's here, and my brave clan will pay their lovely and gentle mistress the adoration due to a divinity." '

But there is a lot to be said for juvenilia. Apart from the entertainment value of its romance, bathos and high good humour – I would hate to have missed the rescue by 'bawling' Dick Crackskull, or the 'man with a red head and ragged inexpressibles' who pops up to solve the barmy plot of this story – it offers a fascinating insight into the author of *Jane Eyre*, *Shirley*, and *Villette*. Charlotte Brontë was hardly more than a child: she had lost her mother at four years old, and two elder sisters; she knew the reality of a harsh school, which later became the Lowood of *Jane Eyre*. She had been well educated as befitted a future governess, but it was all theoretical: at seventeen she had not yet worked for pay, nor travelled out to Brussels (the setting for *Villette*), nor had her talent been recognised by publication. It would be thirteen years before *Jane Eyre* proved that adult life had taught her both honesty and restraint, without quelling the brave spirit of girlhood. By then she had understood that romantic flourishes work better when set against the granite of reality, and that one need not go to a mythical Africa to find the strangeness, endurance and splendour of the human struggle for love.

Yet in this juvenile effort, amid the absurdity, the show-off classical and French tags, and the batty diversion into a dream-story about Napoleon, there are strong clues to solid talent. There is a fertility of images and a passion for description (note the marvellous moonlit woodland, and earlier the idea of the green sea-waves like a plain and the masts of ships like trees, with smaller craft taking 'the form of cattle reposing in their shade'). There is a willingness to let the imagination fly, yet a tartness of riposte which brings *Jane Eyre* irresistibly to mind – the 'vermined slop' of bad food, or the venomous portrait of Colonel the Honourable Alexander Augustus Percy, he of the deceitful mouth and villainous smile. The settings are exotic, yet the observation of the Yorkshire parsonage girl is true when she gets into the countryside and sees the 'illegal rare lads' and 'straightish-legged gentlemen' walking out after a night's poaching or before a good break-fast. The old hag Bertha, with her malignant eye and rusty keys, is pure Brontë: half nightmare and half realistic observation as she mumbles reluctance to house her guest in the tower chambers: 'Nobody's slept in them for more than sixty long years. But what have you brought such a painted toy as this here for? There's no good in the wind, I think'. So is the abductor's reply: 'Silence, you old witch, or I'll cut your tongue out!'

This Charlotte already wanted adventure, and salty exchanges, and peril, and adversity to defy with fledgling courage. And, like all young ladies of spirit who have led sheltered lives, she dearly loved to go slumming in her imagination, relishing every syllable as she writes about 'the favourite abode of briefless lawyers, non-commissioned officers, unpatronised authors, with others of the tag, rag and bobtail species'.

It is novelettish. It is Gothic. It is funny, not always (but sometimes) intentionally. But the main thing is that it connects us, with a rare and rough directness, to the unpolished talent of a writer who we can now know all better for having met her so young.

*– Libby Purves, 2003*

# The Green Dwarf

I am informed that the world is beginning to express in low, discontented grumblings its surprise at my long, profound, and (I must say) very ominous silence.

'What,' says the reading public, as she stands in the market-place with grey cap and ragged petticoat the exact image of a modern blue[1], 'what is the matter with Lord Charles? Is he expiflicated by the literary captain's lash? Have his good genius and his scribbling mania forsaken him both at once? Rides he now on man-back through the mountains of the moon or – mournful thought! – lies he helpless on a sickbed of pain?'

The last conjecture, I am sorry to say, is, or rather was, true. I have been sick, most sick. I have suffered dreadful indescribable tortures arising chiefly from the terrible remedies which were made use of to effect my restoration. One of these was boiling alive in what was called a hot-bath, another roasting before a slow fire, and a third a most rigid system of starvation. For proof of these assertions apply to Mrs Cook, back of Waterloo Palace, situated in the suburbs of Verdopolis[2]. How I managed to survive such a mode of treatment, or what the strength of my victorious constitution must be, wiser men than I am would fail in explaining. Certain it is, however, that I did at length get better or, to speak more elegantly, become convalescent, but long after my cadaverous cheek had begun to reassume a little of its wonted freshness I was kept penned up in a corner of the housekeeper's parlour, forbidden the use of pen, ink and paper, prohibited setting foot into the open air, and dieted on rice-gruel, sago, snail soup, panada, stewed cockchafers, milk-broth and roasted mice.

I will not say what was my delight when first Mrs Cook deigned to inform me, about two o'clock on a fine summer afternoon, that as it was a mild warm day I might take a short walk out if I pleased. Ten minutes sufficed for arraying my person in a new suit of very handsome clothes, and washing the accumulated dirt of seven diurnal revolutions of the Earth from my face and hands.

As soon as these necessary operations were performed, I sallied out in plumed hat and cavalier mantle. Never before had I been fully sensible of the delights of liberty – the suffocating atmosphere which filled the hot, flinty street was to me as delicious as the dew-cooled and balm-breathing air of the freshest twilight in the wildest solitude. There was not a single tree to throw its sheltering branches between me and that fiery sun, but I felt no want of such a screen as with slow, but not faltering step, I crept along in the shadow of shops and houses. At a sudden turn the flowing ever-cool sea burst unexpectedly on me. I felt like those poor wretches do who are victims to the disease called a calenture[3]. The green waves looked like wide-spread plains covered with foam – white flowers and tender spring grass and the thickly clustered masts of vessels my excited fancy transformed into groves of tall, graceful trees, while the smaller craft took the form of cattle reposing in their shade.

I passed on with something of that springing step which is natural to me, but soon my feeble knees began to totter under the frame which they should have supported. Unable to go further without rest, I looked round for some place where I might sit down till my strength might be *un peu retabli*[4]. I was in that ancient and dilapidated court, called (pompously enough) Quaxmina Square, where Bud, Gifford, Love-dust and about twenty other cracked old antiquarians reside. I determined to take refuge in the house of the first mentioned, as well because he is my most intimate friend as because it is in the best condition.

Bud's mansion is indeed far from being either incommodious or unseemly. The outside is venerable and has been very judicially repaired by modern masons (a step, by the by, which brought down the censure of almost all his neighbours), and the inside is well and comfortably furnished. I knocked at the door; it was opened by an old footman with a reverend grey head. On asking if his master were at home he showed me upstairs into a small but handsome room. Here I found Bud seated at a table surrounded by torn parchments and rubbish, and descanting copiously on some rusty knee-buckles which he held in his hand, to the Marquis of Douro, and another puppy, who very politely were standing before him with their backs to the fire.

'What's been to do with my darling?' said the kind old gentleman as I entered. 'What's made it look so pale and sickly? I hope not chagrin at Tree's superannuated drivel.'

'Bless us!' said Arthur, before I could speak a word. 'What a little chalky spoon he looks! The whipping I bestowed on him has stuck to his small body right well. Hey Charley, any soreness yet?'

'Fratricide!' said I. 'How dare you speak thus lightly to your half-murdered brother! How dare you demand whether the tortures you have inflicted continue yet to writhe his agonised frame!'

He answered this appeal with a laugh intended, I have no doubt, to display his white teeth, and a sneer designed to set off his keen wit, and at the same instant he gently touched his riding-wand.

'Nay, my lord,' said Bud, who noticed this significant manoeuvre, 'let us have no more of such rough play. You'll kill the lad in earnest if you don't mind.'

'I'm not going to meddle with him yet,' said he. 'He's not at present in a condition to show game. But let him offend me again as he has done, and I'll hardly leave a strip of skin on his carcass.'

What brutal threats he would have uttered besides I know not, but at this moment he was interrupted by the entrance of dinner.

'My lord and Colonel Morton,' said Bud, 'I hope you'll stay and take a bit of dinner with me, if you do not think my plain fare too coarse for your dainty palates.'

'On my honour, Captain,' replied Arthur, 'your bachelor's meal looks very nice, and I should really feel tempted to partake of it had it been more than two hours since I breakfasted. Last night – or rather this morning – I went to bed at six, and so it was twelve before I rose. Therefore dining, you know, is out of the question till seven or eight o'clock in the evening.'

Morton excused himself on some similar pretext, and shortly after, both the gentlemen – much to my satisfaction – took their leave.

'Now Charley,' said my friend, when they were gone. 'You'll give me your company, I know, so sit down on that easy chair opposite to me, and let's have a regular two-handed crack.'

I gladly accepted this kind invitation because I knew that if I returned home, Mrs Cook would allow me nothing for dinner but a basin full of some filthy vermined slop. During our meal few words were spoken, for Bud hates chatter at feeding-time and I was too busily engaged in discussing the most savoury plateful of food I had eaten for the last month and more to bestow a thought on anything of less importance. However, when the table was cleared and the dessert brought in, Bud wheeled the round table nearer the open window, poured out a glass of sack[6], seated himself in the cushioned armchair, and then said in that quiet, satisfactory tone which men use when they are perfectly comfortable: 'What shall we talk about Charley?'

'Anything you like,' I replied.

'Anything?' said he. 'Why, that means just nothing, but what would you like?'

'Dear Bud,' was my answer. 'Since you have been kind enough to leave the choice of topic to me, there is nothing I should enjoy so much as one of your delightful tales. If you would but favour me this once I shall consider myself eternally obliged to you.'

Of course Bud, according to the universal fashion of storytellers, refused at first, but after a word of flattery, coaxing and entreating, he at length complied with my request and related the following incidents which I now present to the reader not exactly in the original form of words in which I heard it, but strictly preserving the sense and facts.

— C. Wellesley[7]

## 1

Twenty years since, or thereabouts, there stood in what is now the middle of Verdopolis but which was then the extremity, a huge irregular building called the Genii's Inn. It contained more than five hundred apartments, all comfortably, and some splendidly, fitted up for the accommodation of travellers, who were entertained in this vast hostelry free of expense. It became, in consequence of this generous regulation, the almost exclusive resort of wayfarers of every nation who, in spite of the equivocal character of the host and hostess – being the four chief Genii: Tali, Brani, Emi and Anni[8] – and the despicable villainy of the waiters and other attendants, which notable offices were filled by subordinate spirits of the same species, continually flocked thither in prodigious multitudes.

The sound of their hurrying footsteps, the voice of rude revel, and the hum of business has ceased now among the ruined arches, the damp mouldy vaults, the dark halls, and the desolate chambers of this once mighty edifice which was destroyed in the great rebellion, and now stands silent and lonely in the heart of great Verdopolis – but our business is with the past, not the present day, therefore let us leave moping to the owls and look on the bright side of matters.

On the evening of the 4th of June 1814, it offered rather a different appearance. There had been during that day a greater influx of guests than usual – which circumstance was owing to a grand fête to be held on the morrow. The great hall looked like a motley masquerade. In one part was seated cross-legged on the pavement a group of Turkish merchants who, in those days, used to trade largely with the shopkeepers and citizens of Verdopolis in spices, shawls, silks, muslins, jewellery, perfumes, and other articles of oriental luxury. These sat composedly smoking their long pipes and drinking choice sherbet and reclining against the cushions which had been provided for their accommodation. Near them a few dark sunburned Spaniards strutted with the gravely proud air of a peacock, which bird – according to the received opinion – dares not look downwards lest his feet should break the self-complacent spell which enchants him. Not far from these lords of creation sat a company of round, rosy-faced, curly-pated, straight-legged, one-shoed beings from Stump Island, where that now nearly obsolete race of existences then flourished like the green bay tree.[9] More than a dozen Genii were employed in furnishing them with melons and rice-pudding for which they roared out incessantly.

At the opposite extremity of the hall five or six sallow, bilious Englishmen were conversing over a cup of green tea. Behind them a band of withered messieurs sat presenting each other with fine white bread, peculiarly rich elegant Prussian butter, perfumed snuff, brown sugar, and calico. At no great distance from these half-withered apes, within the great carved screen that surrounded a huge blazing fire, two gentlemen had established themselves before a table on which smoked a tempting dish of beefsteaks with the due accompaniments of onions, ketchup and cayenne flanked by a large silver vessel of prime old Canary[10] and a corresponding tankard of spiced ale.

One of the personages whose good fortune it was to be the devourer of such choice cheer was a middle-aged man who might perhaps have numbered his fifty-fifth year. His rusty black habiliments, powdered wig and furrowed brow spoke at once the scholar and the despiser of external decorations. The other presented a remarkable contrast to his companion. He was in the prime of life, being apparently not more than six or seven and twenty years of age. A head of light brown hair arranged in careless yet tasteful curls well became the pleasing, though not strictly regular features of his very handsome countenance, to which a bright and bold blue eye added all the charms of expression. His form, evincing both strength and symmetry, was set off to the best advantage by a military costume, while his erect bearing and graceful address gave additional testimony to the nature of his profession.

'This young soldier,' said Bud, with a kindling eye, 'was myself. You may laugh, Charley' – for I could not forbear a smile on contrasting the dignified corporation of my now somewhat elderly fat friend with the description he had just given of his former appearance – 'you may laugh, but I was once as gallant a youth as ever wore a soldier's sword. Alack-a-day! Time, troubles, good liquor, and good living change a man sorely.'

'But,' the reader will ask, 'who was the other gentleman mentioned above?' He was John Gifford, then the bosom friend of Ensign Bud as he is now of Captain Bud.

There was a profound silence so long as their savoury meal continued, but when the last mouthful of beef, the last shred of onion, the last grain of cayenne, and the last drop of ketchup had disappeared, Gifford laid down his knife and fork, uttered a deep sigh, and opening his oracular jaws, said, 'Well, Bud, I suppose the fools whom we see here gathered together from all the winds of heaven are come to our Babylonian city for the unworthy purpose of beholding the gauds and vanities of tomorrow.'

'Doubtless,' replied the other. 'And I sincerely hope that you, sir, also will not disdain to honour their exhibition with your presence.'

'*I?*' almost yelled the senior gentleman. 'I – go and see the

10

running of chariots, the racing and prancing of horses, the goring of wild beasts, the silly craft of archery, and the brutal sport of the wrestlers! Art thou mad, or are thy brains troubled with the good wine and nutmeg ale?' Here the speaker filled his glass with the latter generous liquid.

'I am neither one nor t'other, Gifford,' answered Bud. 'But I'll venture to say that forasmuch as you despise those gauds and vanities as you call them, many a better man than you is longing for tomorrow on their account.'

'Ah! And I suppose thou art among the number of those arrant fools?'

'Aye, truly said. I see no shame in the avowal.'

'Don't you indeed! Oh, Bud, Bud… I sometimes hope that you are beginning to be sensible of the folly of these pursuits. I sometimes dare to imagine that you will one day be found a member of that chosen band who, despising the weak frivolities of this our degenerate age, turn studiously to the contemplation of the past, who value, as some men do gold and jewels, every remnant, however small, however apparently trivial, which offers a memento of vanished generations.'[11]

'Goodness, Gifford, how you talk! I like well enough to see Melchizedek's cup[12] for the sacramental wine, the tethers by which Abraham's camels were fastened in their pasture-grounds, or even the thigh bone and shoulder blade of one of our own worthy old giants,[13] even when these latter articles turn out to be the remains of a dead elephant. (Ah, Giff, touched ye there, I see.) But as to making such matters the serious business of my life, why hang me if I think I shall turn to that trade before a round dozen of years have trotted merrily over my head.'

'You speak like one of the foolish people,' replied Giff solemnly, 'but still I glean a handful of comfort from your last words. At some future period you will give serious attention to the grand purpose for which we were all brought into the world.'

'Maybe aye and maybe nay. But whether I do or not, my cherub there, Stingo, seems as if he would have no objection to turn both antiquarian and lawyer already.'

'Ha! What! Is it that same sweet boy whom I saw yesterday at your house, whose young features express a promising solemnity far beyond his tender years?'

'The same, and a sour, squalling, ill-tempered brat it is!'

'My dear friend,' said Gifford, with great earnestness, 'take care that you do not check the unfolding of that hopeful flower. Mind my words, he will be an honour to his country, and here, give him these toys' – taking a number of roundish stones from his pocket – 'and tell him I have no doubt they were used as marbles by the children of the ancient Britons. Doubtless he will know how to value them accordingly.'

'To be sure he will. But, my dear friend, the next time you make Stingo a present, let it be some slight treatise on the law. He is continually hunting in my library for books of that nature and complains that he can scarcely find one of the sort he wants.'

'The angel!' exclaimed Gifford in ecstasy. 'The moment I get home I will send him a complete edition of my compendium of the laws. He shall not long pine in the agonies of inanition.'

'You are very kind,' said Bud, 'but now let us change the subject. I understand that Bravey is to occupy the President's throne tomorrow. I wonder who will be the rewarder of the victors.'

'It is not often that I remember the idle chat which passes in my presence, but I heard this morning that Lady Emily

Charlesworth is to be honoured with that dignity.'

'Is she? That's well. They could not possibly have made a better choice. Why, her beauty alone will give éclat to the whole routine of tomorrow's proceedings. Now, tell me honestly, Giff, do you not think Lady Emily the most beautiful of earthly creatures?'

'She's well enough favoured,' replied Gifford; 'that is her garments ever become her person, but for her mind, I fear it is a waste, uncultivated field which, were it not wholly barren, presents a rank crop of the weeds of frivolity.'

'Prejudiced old prig!' said I angrily. 'Would you have a spiritual essence of divinity like that to wither her roses by studying rotten scrolls and bending over grub-devoured law books?'

'Not precisely so, but I would have her to cultivate the faculties with which Nature hath endowed her by a diligent perusal of abridged treatises on the subjects you mention, carefully digested by some able and judicious man. I myself, when her uncle appointed me her tutor in the more solid and useful branches of a polite education, composed a small work of ten quarto volumes on the antiquaries of England, interspersed with explanatory notes, and having an appendix of one thick volume quarto. If I could have got her to read this little volume carefully and attentively through, it might have given her some insight into the noble science of which I am an unworthy eulogist. But while, by a strange perversion of intellect, she listened to openly and followed obediently the instructions of those trivial beings who taught her the empty accomplishments of music, dancing, drawing, modern languages, etc. etc., while she even gave some occasional odd moments to the formation of flowers and other cunning devices on the borders of silken or fine linen raiment, I alone vainly attempted to lure her on in the honourable paths of wisdom, sometimes by honeyed words of enticement, sometimes by thorny threats of correction. At one time she laughed, at another wept, and occasionally (to my shame be it spoken) bribed me by delusive blandishments to criminal acquiescence in her shameful neglect of all that is profitable to be understood by either man- or womankind.'

'Bravo, Giff!' said Bud, laughing. 'I wish she had boxed your ears whenever you bothered her on such subjects! By the by, have you heard that your fair quondam pupil is about to be married to Colonel Percy?'

'I have not, but I do not doubt the rumour – that's the way of all women. They think of nothing but being married, while learning is as dust in the balance.'

'Who and what is Colonel Percy?' said a voice close behind.

Bud turned hastily round to see who the strange interrogator might be. He started as his eyes met the apparition of a tall, slender form dimly seen by the decaying embers which now shone fitfully on the hearth.

'Friend,' said he, stirring up the fire to obtain a more perfect view of the stranger, 'tell me first who and what you are, who ask such abrupt questions about other people.'

'I,' replied he, 'am a volunteer in the cause of good government and suppressor of rebels, and ere long I hope to be able to call myself a brother-in-arms with you, it being my intention shortly to enlist under the Duke's standard.'

As the unknown gave this explanation, a bundle of brushwood which had been thrown on the half-extinguished fire, kindling to a bright blaze, revealed his person more clearly than the darkening twilight had hitherto permitted it to be seen. He appeared to be full six feet high; his figure, naturally formed on a model of the most perfect elegance, derived additional grace from the picturesque though rather singular costume in which he was attired, consisting of a green vest and tunic reaching a little below the knee, laced buskins, a large dark robe or mantle which hung over one shoulder in ample folds and was partially confined by the broad belt which encircled his waist, and a green bonnet surmounted by a high plume of black feathers. A bow and quiver hung on his back, two knives whose hafts sparkled with jewellery were stuck in his girdle, and a tall spear of glittering steel which he held in one hand served him for a kind of support as he stood. The martial majesty of this imposing stranger's form and dress harmonised well with the manly though youthful beauty of his countenance, whose finely chiselled features and full bright eyes, shaded by clusters of short brown curls, shone with an expression of mingled pride and frankness, which awed the spectator while it won his unqualified admiration.

'Upon my word, friend,' said I, struck with the young soldier's handsome exterior, 'if I were the Duke, I should be well pleased with such a recruit as you promise to be. Pray, may I enquire of what country you are a native, for both your garb and accent are somewhat foreign?'

'You forget,' replied the stranger, smiling, 'that you are my debtor for a reply: my first question remains yet unanswered.'

'Ah, true,' said Bud, 'you asked me, I think, who Colonel Percy might be?'

'I did, and it would gratify me much to receive some information respecting him.'

'He is the nephew and apparent heir of the rich old Duke of Beaufort.'

'Indeed! How long has he paid his address to Lady Emily Charlesworth?'

'For nearly a year.'

'When are they to be married?'

'Shortly I believe.'

'Is he handsome?'

'Yes, nearly as much as you, and into the bargain his manners are those of an accomplished soldier and gentleman, but in spite of all this, he is a finished scoundrel, a haughty, gambling, drinking, unconscionable blackguard.'

'Why do you speak so warmly against him?'

'Because I know him well. I am his inferior officer and have daily opportunities of observing his vices.'

'Is Lady Emily acquainted with his real character?'

'Perhaps not altogether, but if she were, I do not think she would love him less. Ladies look more to external than internal qualifications in their husbands elect.'

'Do they often appear in public together?'

'I believe not. Lady Emily confines herself very much to private life. She is said not to like display.'

'Do you know anything of her disposition or temper? Is it good or bad, close or candid?'

'I'm sure I can't tell you, but there is a gentleman here who will satisfy your curiosity on that point. He was her tutor and should know all about it. Pray, Gifford, favour us with your opinion.'

Gifford, hearing himself thus appealed to, emerged from the dark corner which had hitherto nearly concealed him from view. The stranger started on seeing him, and attempted to muffle his face with one end of the large mantle in which he was enveloped, as if for the purpose of avoiding a recognition. But the worthy antiquary, at no time sharp-sighted, and whose brains at this particular juncture happened to be somewhat muddled by the draughts of spiced ale which he had just been administering to himself with no sparing hand, regarded him with a vacant stare of wonder as he drawled out: 'What's your business with me, Bud?'

'I merely wished to know if you could inform this gentleman what sort of temper Lady Charlesworth had.'

'What sort of temper! Why I don't know. Much the same as other girls of her age have, and that's a very bad one.'

The stranger smiled, gave a significant shrug of the shoulder which seemed to say, 'there's not much to be had from this quarter,' and, bowing politely to the corner, walked away to a distant part of the hall.[14]

When he was gone, the two friends sat silent for some time, but Bud's attention was soon attracted by the sound of a voice apparently employed in reading or recitation proceeding from the group of Frenchmen who were seated at no great distance. He walked towards them. The speaker was a little dapper man dressed in brown coat and waistcoat, and creamcoloured continuations. He was uttering the following words with abundance of action and grimace as Bud came up.

'Well as I was saying, the Emperor got into bed. "Cheveleure," says he to his valet, "let down those window curtains and shut the casement before you leave the room." Cheveleure did as he was told and then, taking up his candlestick, departed. In a few minutes the Emperor felt his pillow becoming rather hard, and he got up to shake it. As he did so, a slight rustling noise was heard near the bed-head. His Majesty listened but all was silent, so he lay down again. Scarcely had he settled into a peaceful attitude of repose when he was disturbed by a sensation of thirst. Lifting himself on his elbow, he took a glass of lemonade from the small stand which was placed beside him. He refreshed himself by a deep draught. As he returned the goblet to its station, a deep groan burst from a kind of closet in one corner of the apartment.

"Who's there?" cried the Emperor, seizing his pistols. "Speak, or I'll blow your brains out!" This threat produced no other effect than a short sharp laugh, and a dead silence followed. The Emperor started from his couch, and hastily throwing on a *robe de chambre* which hung over the back of a chair, stepped courageously to the haunted closet. As he opened the door something rustled. He sprang forward, sword in hand; no soul or even substance appeared, and the rustling, it was evident, had proceeded from the falling of a cloak which had been suspended by a peg from the door. Half ashamed of himself he returned to bed. Just as he was about once more to close his eyes, the light of the three wax tapers which burnt in a silver branch over the mantelpiece was suddenly darkened. He looked up. A black opaque shadow obscured it. Sweating with terror the Emperor put out his hand to seize the bell-rope, but some invisible being snatched it rudely from his grasp, and at the same instant, the ominous shade vanished. "Pooh!" exclaimed Napoleon. "It was but an ocular delusion." "Was it?" whispered a hollow voice in deep mysterious tones, close to his ear. "Was it a delusion, Emperor of France? No, all thou hast heard and seen is sad forewarning reality. Rise, Lifter of the Eagle Standard! Awake, Swayer of the Lily Sceptre! Follow me, Napoleon, and thou shalt see more!" As the voice ceased, a form dawned on his astonished sight. It was that of a tall thin man dressed in a blue surtout edged with gold lace. It wore a black cravat very tightly twisted round its neck, and confined by two little sticks placed behind each ear. The countenance was livid, the tongue protruded from between the teeth, and the eyes, all glazed and bloodshot, starting with frightful prominence from their sockets. "*Mon Dieu!*" exclaimed the Emperor. "What do I see? Spectre, whence comest thou?" The apparition spoke not but, gliding forward, beckoned

Napoleon with uplifted finger to follow. Controlled by a mysterious influence which entirely deprived him of the capability of either thinking or acting for himself, he obeyed in silence. The solid wall of the apartment fell open as they approached, and when both had passed through, it closed behind them with a noise like thunder. They would now have been in total darkness had it not been for a dim blue light which shone round the ghost, and revealed the damp walls of a long vaulted passage. Down this they proceeded with mute rapidity. Ere long a cool refreshing breeze, which rushed wailing up the vault and caused the Emperor to wrap his loose nightdress closer round, announced their approach to the open air. This they soon reached, and Napoleon found himself in one of the principal streets of Paris. "Worthy spirit," said he, shivering in the chill air, "permit me to return and put on some additional clothing; I will be with you again presently." "Forward," replied his companion sternly. He felt compelled, in spite of the rising indignation which almost choked him, to obey. On they went through the deserted streets till they arrived at a lofty house, built on the banks of the Seine. Here the spectre stopped, the gates rolled back to receive them, and they entered a large marble hall which was partly concealed by a curtain drawn across, through the half-transparent folds of which a bright light might be seen burning with dazzling lustre. A row of fine female figures richly attired stood before this screen. Each wore on their heads garlands of the most beautiful flowers, but their faces were concealed by ghastly masks representing death's heads. "What is all this mummery?" cried the Emperor, making an effort to shake off the mental shackles by which he was unwillingly restrained. "Where am I, and why have I been brought here?" "Silence!" said the guide, lolling out still further his black and bloody tongue. "Silence if thou wouldst escape instant death." The Emperor would have replied, his natural courage overcoming the temporary awe to which he had at first been subjected, but just then a strain of wild supernatural music swelled behind the huge curtain which waved to and fro and bellied slowly out as if agitated by some internal commotion or battle of warring winds. At the same moment an overpowering mixture of the scents of mortal corruption, blended with the richest eastern odours, stole through the haunted hall. A murmur of many voices was now heard at a distance. Something grasped his arm roughly from behind, he hastily turned round, his eyes met the well-known countenance of Marie Louise. "What, are you in this infernal place, too?" says he. "What has brought you here?" "Will Your Majesty permit me to ask the same question of yourself?" returned the Empress, smiling. He made no reply – astonishment prevented him. No curtain now intervened between him and the light. It had been removed as if by magic, and a splendid chandelier appeared suspended over his head. Throngs of ladies, richly dressed but without death's-head masks, stood round, and a due proportion of gay cavaliers was mingled with them. Music was still sounding, but it was now seen to proceed from a band of mortal musicians stationed in an orchestra near at hand. The air was yet redolent of incense, but it was incense unblended with stench. "*Bon Dieu!*" cried the Emperor. 'How is all this come about, where in the world is Piche?" "Piche?" replied the Empress; "what does Your Majesty mean? Had you not better leave the apartment and retire to rest?" "Leave the apartment! Why, where am I?" "In my private drawing-room, surrounded by a few particular persons of the Court whom I had invited this evening to a ball. You entered a few minutes since in your nightdress with your eyes fixed and wide open.

I suppose, from the astonishment you now testify, that you were walking in your sleep." The Emperor immediately fell into a fit of the catalepsy, in which he continued during the whole of that night and the greater part of the next day.'

As the little man finished his story, a person dressed in blue and gold uniform bustled through the surrounding crowd of listeners and, touching the narrator with a sort of official staff which he carried in his hand, said: 'He arrests him in the name of the Emperor.'

'What for?' asked the little man.

'What for!' reiterated a voice at the other end of the hall. 'He'll let him know what for. What's the meaning of that scandalous anecdote? he should like to know! To the Bastille with him instantly, incessantly!'

All eyes were turned towards the deliverer of this peremptory mandate, and lo! the identical Emperor himself, in his accustomed green surtout and violet-coloured pantaloons, stood surrounded by about twenty gendarmes engaged in continued and uninterrupted snuff-taking. Everyone's attention was now attracted towards *le grand Napoléon*, and *le pauvre petit conteur* [15] was hurried off to the Bastille without further notice or compassion, as it was now getting very late and the inn was all bustle and confusion in consequence of the excitement occasioned among the guests by the arrival of the illustrious visitor. Bud and Gifford, to whom the Emperor was no novelty, thought proper to take their departure. They walked down the first street together and then, as their roads lay in opposite directions, separated for the night.

## 2

A bright and balmy summer's morning ushered in the first celebrations of the African Olympic Games.[16] At an early hour (as the newspapers say), the amphitheatre was crowded almost to suffocation in every part except the open area, a square mile in magnitude, allotted to the combatants, and those private seats which were reserved for the accommodation of the nobility and other persons of distinction.

The scene of the games was not exactly then what it is now. The houses which surround it on three sides were at that time but newly built; some indeed were but half finished, and a few had only the foundations dug. The lofty hill called Frederick's Crag, which completes the circle on the fourth side and whose summit above the seats is at the present day covered with gardens and splendid private dwellings, was then a sombre forest whose ancient echoes were as yet unviolated by the sound of the woodcutter's axe. The stumps of a few recently felled trees likewise appeared in the midst of the newly cleared arena, but it is a question in my opinion whether, by the vast improvements which have since taken place in the neighbourhood of the amphitheatre, the scene has not lost in picturesque variety what it has gained in grandeur and perfect finish.

On that memorable morning the tall magnificent trees, waving their still dewy arms now towards the blue sky which seemed not far above them and now over the heads of as many peoples, nations, tongues and kindreds as Nebuchadnezzar's decree called together on the plains of Dura[17], flung into the prospect a woodland wildness and sylvan sublimity which, in my opinion, would be a more potent and higher charm than any of the artificial forms of beauty our great city has created in their stead are capable of infusing.

After an hour of anxious expectation, the distant sound of musical instruments announced the approach of the principal personages. Bravey advanced slowly and majestically, followed by a brilliant train of nobles. His tall and imposing person was set off to the best advantage by an ample robe of purple splendidly wrought with gold. He took his seat on the President's throne amid bursts of universal applause. After him came Lady Emily Charlesworth, his niece. The flutes and softer instruments of the musicians breathed a dulcet welcome as the fair rewarder of victors, with a graceful rather than stately tread, moved towards her decorated seat. Her form was exquisitely elegant, though not above the middle size, and as she lifted her long white veil to acknowledge the thunderous applause of the multitude, a countenance was revealed such as painters and poets love to imagine, but which is seldom seen in actual life. The features were soft and delicate, the general complexion transparently fair, but tinged on the cheeks and lips with a clear, healthy crimson hue which gave an idea of vigour and healthy freshness. Her eyes, dark, bright, and full of animation, flashed from under their long lashes and finely pencilled brows an arch, laughing, playful light, which, though it might not perhaps have suited well in a heroine of romance, yet added to her countenance a most fascinating though indescribable charm. At first, as she removed her veil and met the gaze of more than a million admiring eyes, a blush mantled on her beautiful cheeks. She bowed timidly though gracefully, and her white hand trembled with agitation as she waved it in reply to their greeting, but she soon regained her composure. The scene before her awoke feelings of a higher nature in her susceptible mind.

The blue and silent sky, the wild dark forest and the broad glimpse of mountainous country opening far beyond, tinged by the violet hues of distance, contrasted with the mighty assemblage of living and moving beings, the great city and the boundless sea beyond. These circumstances, together with the sound of the music, which now in subdued and solemn but most inspiring tones accompanied the heralds as they summoned the charioteers who were to contest the first prize to approach, could not but kindle in every bosom admiration for the simple sublimity of nature and the commanding magnificence of art.

Three chariots now drew up round the starting post. In the first sat a little man with a head of fiery red hair and a pair of keen, malicious black eyes which kept squinting round the arena and regarding everyone on whom their distorted glances chanced to fall with a kind of low blackguard expression which accorded well with the rest of his appearance and equipment. His chariot was rather out of character when compared with the gorgeousness of all surrounding objects, being in fact neither more nor less than a common spring cart drawn by four of those long-eared and proverbially obstinate animals called asses, whom he alternately held in check by means of a rough straw rope bridle or goaded forward with the assistance of a blackthorn staff pointed at one end.

The occupier of the second chariot was a fashionable, dandified gentleman in pink silk jacket and white pantaloons, whose whole attention seemed absorbed by the management of his four handsome bay charges. His name was Major Hawkins, at that time a celebrated hero of the turf and ring.

But it was the third and last charioteer who excited the most general attention. He was a tall and very handsome young man whose symmetrical form appeared to the utmost advantage as he stood upright on his small light car, gallantly reigning in the proud prancing steeds that seemed, by their loud snorting and the haughty elevation of their stately arched necks, to be conscious of their master's superiority over the other combatants. The countenance of this gentleman was, as I have said, handsome: his features were regularly formed, and his forehead was lofty, though not very open. But there was in the expression of his blue and sparkling, but sinister eyes, and of the smile that ever played round his deceitful-looking mouth, a spirit of deep, restless villainy, which warned the penetrating observer that all was not as fair within as without, while his pallid cheek and somewhat haggard air bespoke at once the profligate, the gambler, and perhaps the drunkard. Such is the description, as well as my poor pen can express it, of Colonel the Honourable Alexander Augustus Percy.

All being now ready, the signal for starting broke from a silver trumpet stationed near the President's throne. The three chariots shot off bravely with the swiftness of arrows, running nearly abreast of each other till near the middle of the course, when, to the surprise of all, the little redheaded gentleman with the asses got ahead of the other two and, by dint of a most vigorous system of pricking, reached the goal two minutes before them. No pen or pencil can give an adequate picture of the deep subdued rage which glowed in Colonel Percy's eye and covered his pale cheek and forehead with a dark red flush of anger. He threw one glance of concentrated malignity on the fortunate winner, and then throwing the reins to a groom who stood near in attendance, leapt from his chariot and mingled with the crowd.

It is not my intention to give a full and detailed account of all that took place on that memorable day. I shall merely glance at the transactions which followed and then proceed to topics more nearly connected with my tale.

The sports of horse-racing, wrestling, and bullfighting

followed, in all of which Colonel Percy was engaged: in the first, his favourite horse, Tornado, carried away the gold chaplet from ten of the most renowned steeds in Verdopolis; in the second, he himself successively overcame five powerful antagonists; and in the third, when everyone else turned in dismay from a mighty red bull of the Byson breed after it had ripped up ten horses and gored their riders to death, he mounted Tornado, and with a red crest waving from his hussar's cap and a scarlet cloak depending from his shoulders, rode courageously into the middle of the amphitheatre. The combat for a long time was dubious, but at length, by a well-aimed stroke, his lance drank the huge monster's heart's-blood, and it fell bellowing to the earth which was crimsoned with its gore.

The last prize now remained to be tried for – it was that of archery. Here, too, Colonel Percy presented himself as a competitor. The mark was a tall white wand set at the distance of sixty feet. Twenty noble members of the Archers' Association, all accounted marksmen of the first order, contended for this prize, but the arrows of all fell either more or less wide of the mark. It now became Colonel Percy's turn. He advanced and discharged a carefully directed arrow which, though it came much nearer than any of the rest, failed also in hitting the appointed mark. The heralds now, according to an established form, demanded if there were anyone among the spectators who would undertake to shame the unsuccessful archers. A dead silence followed this demand, for none thought themselves qualified to attempt an enterprise apparently so impracticable, and the President proceeded to adjudge the prize to him whose arrow had come nearest, in default of a better.

He had scarcely uttered the words when a young man of

a form as noble and majestic as that which the ancients attributed to Apollo advanced from the crowd. His dress and appearance I have described before, for it was that identical stranger who on the previous night had arrived at the Genii's Inn. But now instead of the green bonnet and plume which he then wore, a steel helmet covered his face, and the visor, being closed entirely, covered his features.

'My lord,' said he, approaching the President's throne, 'will you permit me the honour of discharging a single arrow before you and the fair rewarder of victors? I delayed my request till now that I might not deprive Colonel Percy of the prize which justly falls to his lot.'

Bravey readily gave his consent, and the stranger, stationing himself twenty feet further off than the appointed distance, unslung the bow and quiver which hung at his shoulder, chose an arrow, tightened his string, and ere another second had elapsed, the splintering of the white wand proclaimed his triumph and skill. A loud thundering cheer rose from the thousands gazing round, and when it had subsided, Bravey, rising from his seat, declared that he rescinded his former decision regarding the prize, and awarded it to the successful stranger. All eyes now turned to Colonel Percy, but no symptom of mortification or anger appeared either in his countenance or behaviour; on the contrary, he turned immediately to the unknown, and with the most friendly cordiality of manner, congratulated him on his good fortune. His civilities were received, however, with a cold and haughty courtesy which told that they were unwelcome as effectually as the most prompt and decided rejection of them could have done. Still the colonel did not seem piqued, but continued to converse with his unsocial conqueror in the free and unembarrassed strain which was natural to him as a man of the world.

'Upon my word!' observed Ensign Bud, who, with his friend Gifford (for he had persuaded the old gentleman to accompany him to see the games), was seated in the front row of the seats. 'Upon my word, I believe the colonel has some fiendish scheme of revenge in his mind or he would never put on that smooth quiet face.'

'Doubtless,' returned Gifford. 'But who is that fantastically arrayed foreigner? Methinks I have heard a voice like his before, though where or when I cannot for my life call to mind.'

Bud was about to reply, but he was prevented by the loud summons of the heralds and the sudden rich swell of music which burst grandly forth as the victors advanced to the foot of the throne and one by one knelt before Lady Emily Charlesworth, from whose hands they were to receive their recompense.

First came the carroty-locked hero of the cart and asses.

'Sir,' said the lady, as she strove vainly to suppress the smile which his odd appearance excited, 'you have this day gained a miraculous victory over one of the most gallant and high-born gentlemen of Verdopolis and are well worthy of the golden wreath which I thus twine round your illustrious temples.'

'Thank you, madam,' replied he, bowing low. 'The colonel's certainly a rum 'un, but I've matched him well today and if you knew all you'd say so too.'

'I do not doubt your ability to match any man,' she replied, laughing, 'and the colonel, in my opinion, has no reason to be ashamed of his defeat, since it was effected by such a consummate master in the art of overreaching as you appear to be.'

He thanked her again and with another low bow gave place to Colonel Percy.

As he, the claimer of three crowns, knelt gracefully at her feet and whispered some flattering compliment in an undertone, Lady Emily seemed visibly embarrassed. She did not blush, but her forehead, before so open and smiling, grew dark and sad. For a moment she sat silent, as if scarcely knowing how to address him, but, most immediately regaining her self-possession, said in a soft yet firm voice, while with her slender and jewelled fingers she bound the garland among his thickly clustered light brown curls: 'It gives me pleasure to be the instrument of rewarding one who has not found his equal in three ardent contests. I trust our city will have as able a champion in every succeeding anniversary of the African Olympic Games.'

'Fair lady,' replied the colonel, 'your approbation would be worth more to me than the transitory applause of ten thousand times the number that have shouted at my trivial exploits today.'

'Strive to deserve it,' said she, in a low, quick voice, 'and it shall not be withheld!'

The herald now summoned the nameless stranger to draw near. Slowly and half-reluctantly he advanced.

'Shall I bid the attendants to remove your helmet,' asked Lady Emily, smiling.

The unknown shook his head, but made no reply.

'Well,' returned she, playfully, 'you are an uncourteous though a gallant archer. But notwithstanding your refusal to comply with my request, I will acknowledge that I think you worthy of the bright garland which I thus twine amongst the feathers which form your crest.'

He rose, and with a stately inclination of the head, withdrew.

All was now concluded. The first celebration of the African Olympic Games was past, and amid a loud and triumphant peal of warlike music, the mighty assembly of a million souls broke up, and, with a crush and tumult that might have annihilated worlds, left the amphitheatre. This dispersion I need not describe, no lives that I am aware of were lost, but hundreds of bags, pockets, fobs and reticules yielded up their contents in the mêlée, while thousands of sides were bruised almost to mummies by an equal proportion of elbows.

Among the principal sufferers, I am sorry to inform the reader our worthy friend, Mr Gifford, must be reckoned. At the first crush – in spite of Ensign Bud's supporting arm, which was tenderly passed round the excellent antiquary's waist – he fell prone to the ground and, in attempting to rise, got entangled among the extended legs of half a score of French messieurs who, greatly to their own edification, were pursuing their way through the huge press, not on their heels like sensible people, but on their heads. When these gentlemen felt the not-very-slight pressure of Mr Gifford's falling carcass, they testified their sense of its inconvenience by that disagreeable agitation of the limbs called kicking. With the utmost difficulty, and with the loss of his best hat and wig, the lawyer was at length rescued, but he had hardly gone twelve paces when his shoes were trodden from his feet, and five minutes after, his Sunday coat – a rich black plush – was torn violently from his back and borne off by some audacious thief. Groaning and sighing, he, still with the assistance of Bud, continued gradually and painfully to push his way, and had almost cleared the thickest part of the crowd, when a hand was unceremoniously introduced into his breeches pockets and all the contents most dexterously extracted. But I need not trouble the reader with more of the unhappy man's misfortunes. Suffice it to say that he did at length get home and was put to bed with unbroken bones. Hot gruel and brandy, administered in large doses, induced a comfortable night's rest, and next morning when he awoke, he was able to curse all games, whether Greek, Roman or African, in unmeasured terms, and to denounce instant vengeance on all who should hereafter propose attendance on their vanities to him.

## 3

The sun, which had risen so brightly and cheerfully, sank to repose with a magnificence worthy of its glorious advent. A short twilight followed. The sea-billows for a time rolled in a dimly lustrous light to the fading shore. Then came the moon. The evening stars began to look out singly from the soft pure sky, the night wind rose, and before it a few pearly clouds, which had been resting motionless on the horizon, glided away beyond the skirting hills. At this tranquil hour the unknown archer, emerging from a grove on the Niger's shady banks where he had been walking since he left the arena, turned his back to Verdopolis and, striking into a bypath which led up the – at that period – wild valley in which our city lies (for there were then no gardens or palaces and but few cultivated fields to variegate its natural beauties), soon forgot, in the calm evening hush which surrounded him, all remembrance of the scene he had quitted an hour before.

Slowly he entered a little sequestered glen formed by the junction of two lofty hills whose summits were covered with woods, but whose bases, excepting here and there a tall spreading tree, exhibited a green slope of unencumbered pasture-land. He stopped, and leaning on the tall spear which, as I have before mentioned, he carried in one hand, stood a few minutes gazing at the lovely moonlight landscape which surrounded him on every side. Then, drawing a bugle from his belt, he blew a clear, but not loud blast which awoke many faint echoes in the wooden hills above. After a brief interval of expectation, steps were heard approaching, and a figure wrapped in a mantle entered from the opposite end of the valley.

'Andrew,' said the archer, 'is that you, my lad?'

'Yes,' replied a voice, whose shrill childish tones and the speaker's diminutive size announced the tender age of the newcomer.

'Come hither then and show me where you have hid the baggage. I am half dead with hunger for it is a full twelve hours since I have either eaten or drunk.'

Andrew immediately scampered off, and in a few minutes returned with a large portmanteau on his shoulders. He now threw aside the mask, and the bright moonshine revealed the person of a boy who might be about thirteen years of age, though from his countenance he seemed upwards of twenty, the sharp keen features lit by a pair of little quick cunning eyes retaining no traces of that juvenile rotundity which is considered the principal characteristic of a child. His dress was as singular as that of his master, being a short plaided petticoat or kilt and a round cap of the same stuff and laced leather buskins. He speedily unlocked the trunk and took from it a kind of basket, the contents of which, when spread on the smooth sward under the shadow of a magnificent elm tree, formed a supper which no hungry man would have passed by with contempt. There was a couple of cold fowls, a loaf of white bread, some cheese, a bottle of palm wine, a vessel of the purest water which Andrew had procured from a small rivulet which, half hidden by wild flowers, washed the roots of the ancient elm tree as it wandered slowly through the valley. While the archer satisfied the cravings of his own appetite, he did not forget his follower who sat at a little distance, ravenously devouring one of the fowl and a large portion of bread and cheese. When their meal was concluded and the fragments were cleared away, Andrew produced from the trunk a large plaided cloak in which his master wrapped himself, and lying down on the green dewy grass with a moss-grown stone for his pillow, he, as well as the boy who lay at his feet, was soon lulled by the low wind rustling in the leafy canopy and drowsy murmurs of the monotonous stream to a dull and dreamless slumber.

An hour elapsed and they still continued in a state of the most profound repose. The moon, now high in heaven, shone with a silvery clearness that almost transformed night into a fairer noon. In Arthur's words, or something like them, 'all felt the heavenly influence of moonlight's milder day,' when a human step suddenly broke the delicious calm reigning around, and (unromantic incident) the apparition not of:

> *A lady fair and bright*
> *With a crown of flowers and a robe of light*

but of a smart footman in a blue coat with silver epaulettes appeared stealing down from the brow of one of the nearest hills. Softly, almost noiselessly, he advanced to the unsuspecting Andrew and, clapping a gag into his mouth, which happened to be wide open, bore him off kicking and struggling in his arms. Andrew's abduction, however, did not last long. An hour had scarcely passed before he returned alone and, without awakening his master to inform him of what had occurred, he lay down in his former place, and in a few minutes was as fast asleep as ever.

The bursting sunlight and singing birds aroused the archer just as the first beams broke forth in summer splendour. Springing lightly from his hard couch, he stirred with his foot the still slumbering page.

'Get up, Andrew,' said he, 'and roll out the contents of that truck onto the grass. I must change this outlandish gear before I venture again into the city, so stir yourself, boy, and here help me first to unbuckle this belt. Why,' continued he, as the lad rose up reluctantly, rubbing his eyes and yawning like one overcome with sleep, 'what ails you, child? Have you been disturbed by fairies tonight that you are so sluggish and drowsy in the morning?'

'No, not I,' said Andrew, laughing rather hollowly and fixing his keen eyes on his master's face as if he would have penetrated to his inmost thoughts. 'No, but I've been troubled with some ugly dreams.'

'Ugly dreams? You little idiot! What were they about?'

'About selling my soul to the old gentleman.[18]

'Well, did you complete the bargain?'

'Yes, and sealed it with a written oath.'

'Come, that was managing the affair in a business-like way – but now a truce to your nonsense, sir, and help me on with this strait waistcoat.'

In a few minutes the archer had stripped off his becoming though peculiar dress and assumed in its stead a fashionable suit of clothes consisting of a blue frock coat which had something of a military air, and white waistcoat and pantaloons.

'Now,' said he, when he had completed his toilet. 'Do you stay here, Andrew? I am going to the city and shall most probably be back before evening. Keep close in the wood till I return and speak to no mortal creature.'

Andrew loudly promised his implicit obedience, and his master took his departure.

The archer in his new costume displayed none of that awkwardness which people usually feel when attired in a novel garment for the first time. On the contrary, it was evident from the perfect ease and grace of his movements, which all partook of a lofty and martial character, that he was not unaccustomed to such a mode of dress. With a slow, melancholy step, he retraced the winding bypath by which he had ascended the valley on the previous evening. The passengers he met were few and far between, for in those days it was a road but little frequented. Two or three milkmaids singing on their way and a few illegal rare lads who were returning from poaching overnight among the hills, together with five or six straightish-legged gentlemen, 'wahking out befahr braukfast to get an auppetite to de Melons and brahd and bautter,' were the only persons with whom he exchanged a morning's salutation, and these did not make their appearance till the latter end of his walk.

At about eight o'clock he reached Verdopolis. Entering at the north gate he proceeded through a series of streets, squares, rows and alleys, along which even at this early hour the living stream of population had begun to flow rapidly, till he reached a quiet street leading from Monmouth Square, formed by two rows of respectable-looking houses whose white window curtains and green Venetian blinds proclaimed the comfortable circumstances of those who inhabited them. Halting at the twelfth mansion, he gave a rousing alarm by means of the well-scoured bright brass knocker. In about two minutes the door was opened by a clean-looking elderly dame, who, the moment she caught a glimpse of our hero's person, uttered a loud exclamation of surprise.

'Bless us, Mr Leslie!' cried she. 'Is that you? Lord, my poor eyes never thought to see your handsome face again.'

'It is me indeed, Alice, but how is your master? Is he at home?'

'At home? Yes indeed, where else should he be, I wonder, when you're standing at his door? But come in, and I'll run to tell him the good news this minute.'

Here the good woman led the way forward, and showing

Mr Leslie into an apartment, ran off to do her errand.

The room into which she had ushered him was a middle-sized parlour, comfortably and even elegantly furnished. A bright fire was burning in the polished steel bars of a handsome grate, and all the paraphernalia of a good breakfast appeared spread on a snow-white damask cloth which covered a round table in the centre of the room. But what principally attracted the eye was a number of very beautiful oil paintings, principally portraits, arranged with judgement on the walls. All betrayed the hand of a genuine master in the art, and some were executed with surprising grace and delicacy. The visitor's countenance expressed something like astonishment as he looked carefully around, but his attention was soon attracted by the unclosing of the door. He started up and stepped eagerly forward as a young man, rather above the middle size, with a pale but interesting countenance and large, intelligent black eyes, entered.

'Well, my dear Frederick,' said he, 'I need not enquire how you are. Your appearance and that of the house tells me, and I suppose I have now only to congratulate you on Fortune's altered disposition.'

'My noble benefactor!' began Frederick de Lisle, while a flush of joy suffused his colourless cheek. 'How I rejoice to see you once again! Are you still Mr Leslie, the artist, or may I now be permitted to address you as –'

'No, no,' interrupted his guest, 'let Leslie be my name for the present. But, Frederick, you must have made a good use of the small sum I gave you if it has entitled you to reside in such a comfortable house as this.'

'Yes,' replied the young man. 'I think I may fairly claim the praise of having employed it to the best advantage, yet it was not that alone which has obtained me the affluence I now enjoy. Your Lordship must know that about three years since, I fell in love (to use the common phrase) with a young and very lovely girl who soon appreciated the sincerity of my affection and returned it. Obstacles, however, apparently insurmountable, opposed our union. Her parents were rich, and they disdained to unite their daughter to a man whose whole wealth lay in a brush and palette.

'For a long time Matilda wept and entreated in vain, but at length her altered looks, her pallid cheek, and her attenuated form so far moved their compassion that they promised to sanction our marriage on condition that I should previously free myself from the pecuniary embarrassment in which I was then entangled. This however was impossible. I had scarcely sufficient employment to procure bread, and as to laying by anything, that was not to be thought of. At this wretched period Your Lordship condescended to become my pupil. The liberal salary which you paid me enabled me to discharge my debts in part, and by the aid of your further munificent gift when you left Verdopolis, I ultimately cleared the whole. My dear Matilda's parents kept their word, and about six months since, I was made the happiest of men. Employment has since poured in rapidly upon me, and I trust that fame – the meed for which I have striven so long and perseveringly under distress and difficulties which might have daunted the spirit of a saint – will at length reward my unwearied endeavours.'

Here the door opened again and Mrs de Lisle entered. She was a young and elegant woman with a pretty face and very genteel manners. Her husband introduced our hero to her as 'Mr Leslie, the gentleman of whom you have often heard me speak'. She curtsied and replied, with a significant smile, 'I have indeed, and the pleasure of seeing him in my house is as great as it was unexpected.'

All three now sat down to a substantial breakfast of coffee, eggs, ham, and bread and butter. The conversation during this meal was animated and interesting, Mrs de Lisle joining in it with a propriety and good taste which did honour to Frederick's choice of a wife. When it was over she left the room, pleading as an excuse for her absence the necessity of attending to household concerns. The two gentlemen, being thus left alone, recommenced the conversation in which they had been engaged before breakfast. Presently, however, they were again interrupted by the arrival of a carriage and the entrance of Alice, who announced Colonel Percy and Lady Emily Charlesworth.

'Ah,' said de Lisle, 'this is fortunate. Your Lordship, I think, will recollect Lady Emily. She used to come often when you painted at my house, and would sit for hours conversing with you about the fine arts. But, my lord, what is the matter – are you ill?'

'No, Frederick,' replied Leslie, though the deadly paleness which overspread his countenance seemed to contradict the truth of what he said. 'Merely a sudden pain in the head to which I am subject. It will soon pass off, but in the meantime I should not like to be seen by these strangers. Will they come into this apartment?'

'No, I have ordered them to be shown into my studio. Lady Emily is come to sit for her portrait which I am painting for Colonel Percy, to whom it is said she is shortly about to be united. They will make a fine couple. Pity the colonel is not as good as he is handsome.'

'De Lisle,' said Leslie, quickly, 'I think it would amuse me if I could watch you paint this morning, but at the same time, I should like to remain concealed myself. Can you not contrive some means of effecting this?'

'Easily, my lord. The library window looks into my studio. You may sit there and entertain yourself as you like.'

'Come then,' returned Leslie, and both left the room together.

The library into which de Lisle conducted his guest was a small apartment furnished with a few well-chosen books principally of the belles-lettres class. One window looked into a little garden at the back of the house, and the other, partially shaded by a green curtain, formed a post of observation by which the studio might be easily reconnoitred. Here Leslie placed himself. The blood returned in full force to his pale cheek as he beheld Lady Emily – more beautiful than he had seen her at the games – reclining gracefully on a sofa. A large velvet carriage mantle trimmed with costly fur fell in rich folds from her shoulders. Her hat, which was ornamented with a splendid plume of ostrich feathers, she had laid aside, and her hair, turned up behind and fastened with a gold comb, fell down on each side of her face in a luxurious profusion of glossy brown ringlets. She was quietly arranging the collar of a small silken-haired spaniel which lay on her lap, and appeared to take little notice of the passionate protestations of the colonel, who was kneeling devotedly beside her. This circumstance, however, was unnoticed by Leslie. He marked only the attitude of both, and an indignant frown darkened his lofty brow. Their love conference, however, (if such it was,) was soon interrupted by the entrance of de Lisle.

'Good morning,' said he, bowing low.

'Good morning,' replied Colonel Percy. 'Now, sir, call up all your skill, summon inspiration to your aid, for the beauty you have to depict is not earthly but heavenly.'

'I hope,' replied the artist, as he seated himself at his easel and began to touch the lovely, though still unfinished resemblance which was placed there, 'I hope you do not consider the attempt I have already made quite a failure.'

'No, not quite. But, Mr Painter, surely you have not the vanity to imagine that an imitation in oil and earths, however skilfully managed, can equal the bright reality of such a form and face as that you have now before you?'

'Do you mean yourself, colonel, or me?' enquired the fair sitter, slyly.

'You, to be sure. Why do you ask the question?'

'Because you gave so many furtive glances into that mirror that I thought your glowing panegyric must have been designed for the figure therein reflected.'

'Hum, I was merely admiring the countenance of a tolerably good-looking monkey which I saw peering through that window at you, and which, by the by, I have seen before in your company, de Lisle.'

Lady Emily turned to the point indicated, but nothing was now visible. She continued to sit for about two hours, then, becoming weary of a compulsory state of inactivity, she ordered the carriage to be called, and together with her escort, Colonel Percy, departed.

## 4

Clydesdale Castle, the seat of the Marquis of Charlesworth, was one of the few mansions which at that period adorned the Glass Town Valley. It was a large and magnificent structure erected during the time of the Second Twelves[19]. The architecture was not of the light Grecian cast in which our modern villas are built, but grand and substantial. Tall arched windows lit the lofty turrets, and pillared Norman gateways gave entrance to the numerous vast halls which were contained under its enbattled roof.

The noble proprietor of this feudal residence was uncle and guardian to the beautiful Lady Emily Charlesworth whose parents, dying when she was yet a child, committed her with their last breath to the protection of her only surviving relative[20]. This trust the Marquis discharged faithfully, as the reader may perceive from the circumstance of his having appointed John Gifford Esquire tutor to his niece, and she in return regarded him with that affection which an amiable mind will always cherish towards those from whom it has received any benefit.

About a week after the time mentioned in my last chapter, Lady Emily was sitting one afternoon in her solitary chamber in the west turret. She was alone. Her elbow rested on the little work table beside her, and her full dark eyes were fixed with an expression of deep melancholy on the blue and far-distant mountain boundary which appeared through the open lattice. I cannot tell what she was thinking of, for I never heard, but soon a few tears trickling down her soft cheek betrayed that her meditations belonged rather to *Il Penseroso* than *L'Allegro*.[21] These mute monitors seemed to rouse her from her sad reverie. With a deep sigh she turned away from the window and, drawing a harp towards her which stood near, began to sing in a sweet low voice the following *petit chanson*[22]:

*The night fell down all calm and still;*
*The moon shone out o'er vale and hill,*
*Stars trembled in the sky.*
*Then forth into that pale, sad light*
*There came a gentle lady bright,*
*With veil and cymar spotless white,*
*Fair brow and dark blue eye.*

*Her lover sailed on the mighty deep,*
*The ocean wild and stern;*
*And now she walks to pray and weep*
*For his swift and safe return.*

*Full oft she pauses as the breeze*
*Moans wildly through those giant trees,*
*As startled at the tone*
*The sounds it waked were like the sigh*
*Of spirits' voice through midnight sky,*
*So soft, so sad so drearily,*
*That wandering wind swept on:*

*And ever as she listened,*
*Unbidden thoughts would rise,*
*Till the pearly tear-drop glistened,*
*All in her star-like eyes.*

*She saw her love's proud battleship*
*Tossed wildly on the storm-dark deep,*

*By the roused wind's destroying sweep,*
*A wrecked and shattered hull.*
*And as the red bolt burst its shroud*
*And glanced in fire o'er sea and cloud,*
*She heard a peal break deep and loud,*
*Then sink to echoes dull.*

*And as that thunder died away,*
*She saw amid the rushing spray,*
*Her Edward's eagle plume.*
*While thus that deadly scene she wrought,*
*And viewed in the dim realms of thought,*
*His soul's appalling doom,*

*A voice through all the forest rang,*
*Up like a deer the lady sprang:*
*' 'Tis he, 'tis he,' she cried,*
*And ere another moment's space*
*In time's unresting course found place,*
*By Heaven! and by Our Lady's grace,*
*Lord Edward clasped his bride.*

The song was ended, but her fingers yet lingered among the harp-strings from which they drew long wailing notes, whose plaintive sound seemed all unsuited to the happy termination of the romance she had just been warbling. The tears she had before checked were now suffered to flow freely, and faint sobs were beginning to reveal the secret grief which oppressed her, when suddenly the door opened and a servant entered with the intelligence that a gentleman had arrived who wished to see her ladyship.

'A gentleman!' exclaimed Lady Emily, wiping her eyes and

trying to assume some degree of composure. 'What is he like? Have you ever seen him before?'

'Never, my lady. He is a personable young man with a very piercing look.'

'Did he not tell you his name?'

'No, I asked him what it was but he gave me no answer.'

'That is strange. Is he alone, or accompanied by servants?'

'He has one little page with him but that is all.'

'Well, show him into my drawing-room and say that I will be down directly.'

The servant bowed and withdrew. Lady Emily now hastened to remove the traces of recent tears. She bathed her face in water, carefully arranged her dress, and smoothed her dishevelled ringlets. Having thus discharged the duties of the toilet, she proceeded to attend the unknown visitor.

With a light tread she glided from her apartment, down the staircase, and through a portion of the corridor till she reached the drawing-room. Its rosewood folding doors rolled back noiselessly at her touch on their well-polished hinges, and she entered unobserved by the stranger, whose tall and kingly form stood before her, opposite the great arched window through which he was gazing with folded arms. For an instant she paused to admire the statue-like dignity of his attitude. Her heart, she could not tell why, beat wildly as she looked at him. But fearing that he might turn suddenly and take her unawares, she proclaimed her presence by a gentle cough. He started and turned round. Their eyes met. The pensive expression which had dwelt in Lady Emily's vanished like magic and a brilliant ray of animation sparked in its stead.

'Leslie, dear Leslie,' cried she, springing joyfully towards him. 'Is it you? How long have you been in Verdopolis? Why did you not return long since? Oh, how often have I thought and cried about you since you went away!'

She was going on, but, observing that a cold and haughty bow was the only return her cordial welcome met with, stopped in embarrassment. A mutual silence of some moments followed which was at length broken by Leslie, who stood with his arms folded, gazing earnestly at her.

'Beautiful hypocrite,' said he, and paused again, while his finely cut lip quivered with the strongest emotion.

'What is the matter?' asked Lady Emily, faintly. 'Have I been too forward, too ardent in my expressions of pleasure at seeing you again after so long an absence?'

'Cease this unworthy acting,' said her lover, sternly, 'and do not think so meanly of me as to imagine I can be deceived by pretensions so flimsy. You have been too well employed during my absence to think much of me. Another and – doubtless in your opinion – a higher prize has been ensnared by your false, though incomparable, loveliness, and now I am come to cast you from me as a perjured woman, though my heartstrings should burst in agony from the effort. But,' he continued, in a voice of thunder, while all the lightnings of jealousy gleamed in his fierce dark eyes, 'I will not tamely give you up to the scoundrel who has dared to supplant me. No! He shall have an even struggle, he shall wade through blood to obtain his stolen reward.'

'Leslie, Leslie,' replied Lady Emily, in a soft soothing tone. 'You have indeed been deceived, but not by me. Sit down now calmly and tell me all you have heard to my disadvantage. You see I am not angry, notwithstanding this is a far different reception to what I had ever expected to meet with from you.'

'Siren,' said her yet unappeased lover, 'who would imagine that so sweet a voice could be employed in the utterance of falsehoods, or that such a lovely countenance should be a mere mask to conceal the hollow insincerity of a coquette's heart.'

Lady Emily, whose fortitude was unequal to sustain this continued severity, now burst into tears. Leslie, deeply moved by her distress, whether real or apparent, began to reflect what right he had to upbraid her in such haughty terms, and to ask himself whether the reports which had awakened his suspicions might not be in themselves destitute of foundation.

Under the influence of these thoughts he approached the sofa on which she had thrown herself when unable to stand from excess of agitation, and sitting down beside her, took her hand, but she withdrew it with becoming pride.

'Mr Leslie,' said she, starting up, 'your words show the regard you once pretended to entertain for me is no more. You desire that we should part. And be assured that whatever pain I may experience in renouncing one whom I have hitherto looked upon as my dearest friend, yet I shall not hesitate a moment to take this necessary though painful step. Farewell, then, I trust that the bitterness of remorse for wrongs inflicted upon others will never be added to your portion of this world's evils.'

As she spoke the blood rushed to her terror-blanched cheek, her tearful eye shone like a meteor, and her slender form seemed dilated with the swell of justly aroused pride. Leslie sat silent till she turned to depart, then springing from his seat he hastily placed himself between her and the door.

'You shall not go,' said he. 'I am convinced that I was mistaken. The man who could hear your words and look on your countenance would be more or less than human if he could still doubt that you were innocent.'

Lady Emily continued to advance with an irresolute step, but a smile now began to dimple her fair cheek.

'Well, Leslie,' she said, 'you are – like a true artist – one of the most capricious of men. But this moment you were so angry with me that I was almost afraid to remain in the room, and now you will not let me leave. But –' she continued, while the arch smile more fully lit up her face, 'perhaps I shall not choose to remain now. I really am very angry, and feel a great mind to tell Colonel Percy next time he comes (for I suppose he is the person you are jealous of) that I have cut his rival and shall marry him forthwith.'

'Hush, Emily,' replied Leslie, leaving his post near the door. 'I cannot bear to hear you speak thus, even in jest. But come, let us sit down, and tell me seriously who and what is the wretch whose name has just passed your lips.'

'He is a very handsome and accomplished man,' she replied, provokingly, 'and my uncle says one of the bravest soldiers in the army.'

Leslie's eyes flashed and his brow darkened again. 'Am I to think,' he asked, 'that you entertain a partiality for the infamous villain?'

'Goodness,' exclaimed the lady, 'can't I like two people at once? How monopolising you are!'

The convulsive grasp with which her lover seized her hand and the flush which rose suddenly to his cheek warned her that she had trifled long enough. She proceeded in an altered tone: 'But though the colonel is all I have described him, yet I assure you, you have nothing to fear, for I detest him most thoroughly and nothing on earth should either tempt or compel me to change my name from Emily Charlesworth to Emily Percy.'

'Bless you!' exclaimed the enthusiastic Leslie, 'for that assurance! It has relieved me of a mighty load. But tell me, dearest, how these vile reports by which I have been misled arose. Colonel Percy, I presume, has visited you?'

'He did, and made proposals to me, but I remembered the absent, and peremptorily rejected him. He then applied to my uncle who, as ill luck would have it, behaved like all guardians and commanded me forthwith to receive him as my husband elect. I demurred, my uncle insisted, the colonel implored. Hints of compulsion were thrown out. This only served to render me more restive. The chaplain was sent for. I then had recourse to tears. The colonel, seeing me so far softened, became a little insolent. He said that instead of crying and pouting, I might think myself very highly honoured by the preference of one whom all the ladies in Verdopolis would be glad of. This effectually awoke my spirit. I got up, for I had been kneeling to both the oppressors, and told him that he was the object of my scorn and hatred and that he never need hope to obtain any interest in a heart that was entirely devoted to another. When he heard this he stormed and frowned, just as you did just now. My uncle asked who the favoured suitor was. I said instantly that he was neither lord nor knight, but a young and gifted artist. If you had seen the fit of astonishment that seized them both! They stood with mouths gaping and eyes staring like two images of surprise. The effect was perfectly ludicrous, and despite of the fears which filled me, I laughed outright. This only irritated them still more. The colonel swore that he would compel me to marry him or die, and my uncle took oath on belt and brand that no man from king to beggar, from duke to artist, should be my husband except Colonel Percy. I smiled but said nothing. Well, for a while after this I was confined to my room and not suffered to cross the threshold lest I might run away. This rigour injured my health – I grew pale and thin. My uncle (who I know loves me, notwithstanding his harshness) perceived the change and

49

commanded that I should be set at liberty on condition of my consenting to accompany the colonel for the purpose of having my portrait taken. The first time I went to de Lisle's in order to sit, Colonel Percy told me that he had discovered who my lover was and had even seen him several times. This frightened me a little but I consoled myself with the knowledge that you were at present absent from Verdopolis and therefore out of his reach, but now you are returned I fear greatly that he will never rest till he has accomplished your destruction by some means.'

'Emily,' said Leslie, as she concluded her brief narrative, 'you have acted generously and truly. You have been faithful to a poor and friendless artist – or one whom you thought such – and have rejected a man whose birth, expectations, and personal accomplishments render him an object of the highest admiration to every other individual of your own sex. I now know with a degree of certainty which admits no shadow of a doubt that you love me for myself, and that nothing of a selfish nature mingles with your regard. I owe it therefore to your disinterested affection to reveal my real rank and station in life. I am not what I seem – a servile minion of fortune, a low-born son of drudgery. No, the head of Clan Albyn, the Earl of St Clair, the Chieftain of the wild children of the mist, descends from a line of ancestors as illustrious as any whose brows were ever encircled by the coronet of nobility. Alliance with me will not bring you to want and beggary, but pure blood will be mingled, broad lands joined, and loving hearts united in bonds dissoluble only by death. Come with me then, Emily, shake off at once the shackles which restrain you! Free yourself from the importunities of a villain! I will take you to my mountainous lands in the north, and you shall be at once Countess of St Clair and lady of seven thousand of the bravest warriors that ever gathered round a chieftain's banner. My castle on Elimbos is larger than your uncle's here, and my brave clan will pay their lovely and gentle mistress the adoration due to a divinity.'

As Leslie, or as we must now call him, Ronald Lord St Clair, revealed his rank and power, the proud blood mounted to his forehead, his eye flashed like that of one of his own wild eagles, and the majesty of his step and bearing as he slowly paced the apartment proclaimed the descendant of a hundred earls. Lady Emily caught the lofty enthusiasm which infused a higher beauty into his noble countenance and, rising from her seat, she frankly extended her hand towards him and said, 'Accept the pledge of my inviolable faith. Though the whole earth should unite against me, I will never love another. "True till death" shall be my chosen motto. I cannot love you more than I did, but I rejoice for your own sake that you can vie in rank with the proudest nobles of Africa.'

'Do you consent to go with me?' asked he.

'I do. At what time must I depart?'

'This night at twelve o'clock meet me in the chestnut avenue.'

'I will be punctual,' said the lady. 'And now, my lord, tell me what your reason was for playing the incognito in Verdopolis.'

'Why, Emily, you must know that I was educated in England. After leaving Oxford, I resided some time in London. There I was, of course, admitted into the highest circles of society; being young and rich, great attention was paid me. The ladies in particular treated me very graciously, but I suspected that much of this special favour was owing rather to my rank and fortune than to my personal qualities. This idea having once entered my head, I could not by any means drive it out. So I determined to take a voyage to Africa and try what luck would befall an unknown and apparently friendless stranger. In Verdopolis I met with de Lisle. His manners and address pleased me, while his merits and poverty excited my warmest sympathy. Enjoining the strictest secrecy, I told him who I was and my motives for wishing to remain unknown. Having some knowledge of painting, I determined to assume the character of an artist, and accordingly placed myself under de Lisle's tuition. At his house I met with you, for you used to come there occasionally under the protection of your worthy tutor, Mr Gifford, to purchase copies and drawing materials. The consequence of these interviews I need not relate. In a short time we became firmly attached to each other, and when I was about to declare my rank and formally to solicit your hand of Lord Charlesworth, I was suddenly called away to my northern estates among the Branni mountains. Legal affairs and business connected with the clan unavoidably detained me for nearly twelve months, and now I have returned to Verdopolis for the double purpose of claiming you as my bride, and when that is accomplished, joining the Duke of Wellington's standard against the rebellious Ashantees.'

'I have but one more question to ask,' said Lady Emily. 'How did the colonel become acquainted with your person?'

'I know not, except it be by having seen me at de Lisle's house. I remember a gentleman strongly resembling him entering the studio one day when you were conversing with me, and regarding us with an eye of the strictest scrutiny, but the circumstance had slipped my memory until your question recalled it.'

'There still remains a single point on which I wish to be satisfied,' said Lady Emily smiling, as if a sudden thought had struck her. 'Were you present at the Olympic Games in disguise?'

'I was.'

'What dress did you wear?'

'The costume of my clan.'

'Then you were the gallant archer whose arrow shivered the white wand when every other failed.'

'You have guessed cleverly, Emily – it is as you say.'

'Then depend upon it, my lord,' said she, seriously, 'Colonel Percy recognised you. His eye is keener than a hawk's, and I saw him glance sharply at you when you half lifted your visor to speak. Could I have heard your voice, I should have remembered it, I am certain, and doubtless he did so. Oh, I fear his vengeful spirit will never rest till it has accomplished your destruction.'

'Fear nothing for me, Emily, my sword is as good as his, and my arm also. If he causes a tear to spring in that bright eye, his heart's blood shall pay for it. And now, my dearest, farewell. We must part for the present, but before another sun rises the conjoined powers of earth and hell will be insufficient to divide us. Only remember the appointed time. Be punctual and trust to me for the rest.'

Lady Emily repeated the promise she had before given, and the lovers separated, each to make the necessary preparations. As Lord St Clair left the drawing-room he saw a shadowy form hastily gliding down the dark corridor. Fearful of their conversation having been overheard, he pursued the retreating figure. At first he appeared to be gaining some advantage, but suddenly it turned down a side passage and he lost sight of it. Chagrined at this failure, and somewhat apprehensive of what this nimble-footed personage's design might be in lurking so suspiciously about, he thought of returning back and acquainting Lady Emily with what he had seen, but just then the Marquis of Charlesworth's gruff, stern voice was heard in the hall, so our hero thought it best to take his departure instantly, lest his presence might be discovered by that dignitary and the whole plan of elopement blown up. He proceeded therefore to the stables where he found both page and horse in readiness. Mounting his beautiful Arabian charger, with one glance at the western turret and one sigh for his lady-love, he dashed out of the yard, and in a few minutes was halfway on the road to Verdopolis.

## 5

For the present I must leave Lord St Clair and Lady Charlesworth to see what Colonel Percy was about while they were preparing to cheat him so cleverly. The colonel occupied a large and splendid mansion in Dim-dim Square, then a fashionable quarter of the city, though now the favourite abode of briefless lawyers, non-commissioned officers, unpatronised authors, with others of the tag, rag and bobtail species. This residence, together with the expensive establishment of servants, carriages, etc. appertaining to it, was kept up partly by the owner's pay, partly by his gains at the billiard- and card-table, and partly by liberal borrowings from usurers on the strength of his great expectations. There, in a magnificent saloon, furnished with all the elegance that luxury or taste could devise, Colonel Percy sat alone on the afternoon spoken of in my last chapter. His fine form was stretched in very unmilitary ease on a silken sofa. His languid eye and pale cheek revealed the dissipation of the previous night, while the empty decanter and glass which stood on a table near him showed that the stimulus of wine had been employed to remove his lassitude, though without effect. While he was lying thus with his hands pressed to his lofty and aristocratic forehead, a window of the saloon was suddenly opened, and a man with a red head and ragged inexpressibles sprang in from without.

'Beast,' said Percy, starting up with a loud oath. 'How dare you enter my house in such a brazenly impudent manner! How dare you come near me in fact after the manner in which you have lately treated me!'

This reception did not in the least seem to daunt the unabashed entrant whom no doubt our readers will have already recognised as the hero of the ass-drawn chariot. On the contrary, he advanced with a smiling countenance and, seizing the colonel's hand with his horny paw, replied, 'How is all with you, my sweet rogue? I'm afraid you're not quite as your best friends could wish – that pale face and this feverish hand tell tales.'

'Curse you for the hardiest scoundrel that ever deserved a hempen neckcloth[23],' replied the colonel, at the same time dashing the other hand into his face with a violence that would have felled any other man, but which only drew a horse-laugh from the sturdy charioteer. 'Curse you ten thousand times, I say! How in the name of body and soul dare you face me alone and without arms after our last transaction?'

'What have I done to thee, my Emperor of Rogues?'

'What have you done to me, brute? Did I not bribe you with two hundred guineas to cut out Captain Wheeler from running his chariot at the games by becoming a competitor yourself with your vile cart and asses? Did I not give you fifty guineas more in advance to let me win? And after swearing a hundred oaths of fidelity did you not break them all, and by so doing swindle me out of twenty thousand pounds, for I had laid a wager to that amount on my success?'

'Well, and if I did all this,' replied the carroty-haired gentleman, 'was it not just what you would have done in my situation? I had your two hundred and fifty pounds safe in my breeches-pocket when by ill or good luck – which you please – as soon as it was publicly known that I was to run, upwards of forty bets were laid against me. I accepted them all, and so in self-defence was obliged to do my best. But come,' he continued, 'this is not what I intended to talk about. My purpose for coming here was to beg the loan of a few hundred pounds. I've spent every farthing of what I got last week in drink and other matters.'

This demand was made in a quiet, self-complacent tone, as if the request had been one of the most reasonable in the world. Colonel Percy could bear it no longer. Quivering all over and deadly pale with rage, he snatched a loaded pistol from his pocket and discharged it full at him. This attack, like the former, produced no other effect than a fiendish laugh. The shot flew from his head, and in the rebound, one of them struck the colonel so smartly as to produce blood. Baffled in this manner a second time, he threw down the weapon and began to pace the apartment with furious strides. 'Fool that I am,' cried he. 'Why do I waste my strength in vain? The demon, as I might have known before now, is impervious to fire or shot. My fruitless attempts only expose me to his derision.'

'Ha, ha, ha,' shouted his tormentor. 'That's true, rogue, so now sit down and let's have a little sensible conversation.'

Percy, exhausted with the efforts he had made, threw himself mechanically into a chair. 'S'death,' said he, in a calmer tone. 'You're not a man. As sure as I live you're an evil spirit in the flesh, a true fiend incarnate. No human being could have lived after a shower of such hailstones as those.'

S'death (for such was the unblushing swindler's name) made no answer, but rising from his seat, went to a sort of buffet or sideboard on which stood several bottles of wine etc., and taking a case of liquors, first helped himself to a brimming bumper and then, pouring out another, advanced with it to Rogue – Percy, I mean.

'Here, charmer,' said he, lifting it to his lips. 'Here, taste this cordial – you look faintish, I think, and should have something to comfort your poor heart.'

The colonel, who at that time was no drunkard, whatever

he may have become since, just sipped of the offered beverage and returned it to Mr S'death by whom it was annihilated at a draught. The conversation was now carried on in a more animated and less violent strain than before. Percy's anger seemed to have been in some measure appeased when he found that it was useless to exert it against one whom he could not possibly injure. Still, however, half at least of every sentence they addressed to each other was composed of oaths and execrations. S'death continued to demand a loan of twenty pounds which Percy for some time refused, declaring that he had not that sum in the world. S'death then tried to intimidate him and threatened to inform against him for certain highly criminal transactions in which he had been concerned. This had the desired effect: the colonel immediately unfastened a diamond clasp from his stock and, throwing it on the floor, commanded him with an oath 'to take that and be off'.

The hardened villain picked it up with a chuckle and, going again to the sideboard, helped himself to another tumbler of liquor. He then made his exit through the open window, saying, as he went away, 'Goodbye, Rogue, at this moment I have bank bills for two thousand pounds in each waistcoat pocket.' With these words he scampered off, followed by the discharge of a second pistol.

'Infernal scoundrel,' said the colonel, as he closed the sash with violence. 'I wish the earth would yawn and swallow him up, or the skies rend and strike him dead with a flash of his native element.'

As he uttered this pious aspiration, he flung himself again on the sofa from which he had been roused by his unwelcome visitor. Two hours elapsed before he was again disturbed, but at the end of that time a low tap was heard at the door.

'Come in, beast, whoever you are,' shouted he in a loud voice.

The door softly unclosed and a footman in livery entered.

'What do you want now scoundrel?' asked his master furiously.

'Merely to tell your honour that the green dwarf has just arrived quite out of breath and says he has important information to communicate.'

'The green dwarf! Show him into my library and say I'll come directly.'

The servant bowed and left the room. Colonel Percy followed him almost immediately and proceeded to the library. There we shall now leave him to revisit Clydesdale Castle.

Lord St Clair had hardly left Lady Emily's private drawing-room before her uncle, the Marquis of Charlesworth, entered it. He was a tall and stately old gentleman, between sixty and seventy years of age. His grey locks, curled and powdered with the most scrupulous nicety, surrounded a countenance whose fresh weather-beaten skin, stern aquiline features, and peculiar expression would have at once marked him out to the attentive observer as a veteran soldier, even if his military jackboots and enormous sword had not done so more decidedly.

'Well, Emily,' said he, saluting his niece who had run forward to meet him. 'How are you this evening, love? I'm afraid you've had a dull day of it, sitting here alone.'

'Oh, no, uncle,' said she. 'I never in the least feel the want of company. My books and music and drawing give me sufficient employment without it.'

'That's well, but I think you have not been quite alone this evening. Has not the colonel been with you?'

'No,' replied Lady Emily. 'Why do you ask me, uncle?'

'Because I saw a very handsome horse standing in the yard which I concluded to be his, but since it was not, pray what other visitor have you had?'

This was an unexpected question. Lady Emily, however, was not thrown off her guard by it. She instantly did what perhaps will not be thought very becoming in the heroine of a novel, viz. coined a little lie.

'Oh,' she said, carelessly, 'I suppose the horse must have belonged to Mr Lustring, the linen-draper's apprentice. He has been here this afternoon with some articles which I bought at his master's shop the other day. And now uncle,' she continued, willing to change the conversation to some less ticklish subject, 'tell me what you have been doing in the city today.'

'Why,' said he, 'in the first place I went to Waterloo Palace for the purpose of soliciting an audience of the Duke. Our interview lasted two hours, and when it was over, His Grace requested my company to dinner. There I saw the Duchess who was as affable and agreeable as ever. She asked kindly after you, and desired me to say that she should be happy to have the pleasure of your society for a few weeks at Verdopolis.'

'Sweet creature!' exclaimed Lady Emily. 'I love her more than anybody else in the world except you, uncle, and perhaps one or two besides. But did you see the little baby?'

'Yes.'

'Is it a pretty child?'

'Remarkably so, but I fear it will be spoiled. The Duke seems disposed to indulge it in everything, and the Duchess' whole existence is evidently wrapped up in it.'

'And no wonder. Pray, what's it called?'

'Arthur, I believe.'

'Does it seem well dispositioned?'

'I really don't know. It will be tolerably headstrong, I think. There was a regular battle between it and the nurse when she attempted to convey it out of the room after dinner. Now, have you any more questions to ask concerning this little imp?'

'Not at present. What did you do when you left the palace?'

'I stepped into the Genii's Inn and had a bottle of wine with Major Sterling. After that I proceeded to our barracks where I had some business to transact with the officers of my regiment. When this was finished, I went to Mr Trefoil's and purchased something for my niece to wear on her wedding day, which I intend shall arrive soon.'

Here the Marquis took from his pocket a small casket in which, when it was opened, appeared a superb diamond necklace with earrings, finger-rings and broaches to correspond. He threw them into Lady Emily's lap. A tear started into her eye as she thanked him for this costly present, and at the same time thought what an act of disobedience to her kind uncle's will she was about to commit.

He observed it and said, 'Now, my love, let us have no piping. The colonel is an admirable fellow, a little wild perhaps, but marriage will soon cure him of that.'

A long silence followed; both uncle and niece, judging by their pensive countenances, seemed to be engaged in sorrowful reflections. At length, the former resumed the conversation by saying, 'In a few days, Emily, we shall have to be separated for some time.'

'How?' exclaimed Lady Emily, starting and turning pale, for her thoughts instantly reverted to Colonel Percy.

'Why my love,' replied the Marquis, 'news has lately arrived that the Ashantees are mustering strong. The Duke therefore considers an addition to the army requisite. Several regiments have been ordered out as reinforcements among which number is the ninety-sixth, and, I being commander, must of course accompany it. It is on this account that the Duchess of Wellington has invited you to pay her a visit for she very kindly considers that you will feel Clydesdale Castle a very dull and lonely residence in my absence. I hope you will accept the invitation, my love.'

'Certainly,' replied Lady Emily, in a faint voice, for her heart misgave her when she thought of the deceitful part she was acting towards the careful and affectionate guardian from whom she was about to be separated perhaps for ever.

Supper was now announced and when this meal was concluded, Lady Emily, pleading a slight headache as an excuse for retiring early, bade her uncle goodnight, and with a heavy heart, proceeded to her little chamber in the western turret. When she reached it and had secured the door, she sat down to consider a little of the decisive step she was about to take. After long and deep meditation she arrived at the conclusion that there were but two practicable modes of acting, namely either to obey her uncle, prove false to her lover, and sacrifice her own happiness for life, or to disobey the Marquis, be faithful to St Clair, and run away with him according to her promise.

Driven to such a dilemma, who can blame her if she made a choice of the latter course and determined to run the hazard of an elopement rather than to await the evils which delay might produce. Just as her resolution was fixed, the castle bell began in deep and solemn tones to announce the eventful hour of midnight. Each stroke of the resounding hammer seemed in her excited imagination a warning voice enjoining her instant departure. As the last hollow echo died away to the profoundest silence, she started from the chair where she had hitherto sat motionless as a statue, and proceeded to wrap herself in a large hooded mantle such as was then frequently worn by the ladies of Verdopolis, and which served the treble purpose of a veil, hat and cloak.

Thus attired, she stole noiselessly from her chamber and, instead of proceeding toward the grand staircase, directed her steps to the winding turret stair which led to an unoccupied hall in which was an arched gate opening directly into the park. As she softly entered this hall she perceived, by the moonlight, which was streaming brilliantly through the tall latticed windows, a dark figure standing near the gate through which she was to pass. Lady Emily was not much of a philosopher, and this appearance startled her not a little for she instantly remembered a traditional story of a wicked fairy who was said to haunt this apartment. Her fears on this head, however, were soon relieved by hearing the rattling of a bunch of keys, accompanied by the gruff murmuring tones of a man's voice,

'I wonder,' said the supposed apparition, in soliloquy, 'I wonder what that beast of a light chose to go out for; it's a rare thing, to be sure, for me to be in this dog-hole at midnight without a candle. That last pint made my hand rather unsteady and I can't see to find the keyhole.'

Lady Emily now recognised in the speaker a manservant whose office it was to secure all the castle gates before retiring to rest. The urgency of her situation immediately suggested an expedient which, considering the muddled state of the man's brain, could hardly fail of success. She wrapped herself closely in the mantle and, advancing into the middle of the hall, said, in a voice as commanding as she could muster, 'Mortal, I command thee to depart from the great fairy Asherah's abode.'

The effect of this ruse was instantaneous. He flung down the keys with a shout of terror and scampered off as fast as his heels could carry him. Lady Emily had now no difficulty in unbarring the portal and making her premeditated escape. With the lightness and swiftness of a liberated deer she bounded across the moonlit lawn towards the appointed place of rendezvous.

A chill and dreary wind was sweeping among the lofty chestnut trees as she wandered under their huge boughs, impatiently awaiting her lover's arrival. The uncertain light, now streaming through a wide opening as the swelling breeze suddenly bowed all the branches in one direction, and now, when it died away and they sprang back to their former station, flinging a thousand silvery chequers on the leaf-strewn pathway, produced shadows equally uncertain. Sometimes it seemed as if a hundred ghosts were gliding among the mighty trunks, beckoning with their dim hands and vanishing as she approached them. Occasionally, too, a cloud would suddenly obscure the moon, and then, in the dense darkness which followed, the creaking of the branches, the rustling of leaves, and the wild howling of wind, formed a combination of doleful sounds which might have impressed the stoutest heart with terror.

For half an hour she continued to walk slowly about, shivering in the cold night air and at intervals pausing to listen for some advancing step. At length she heard a rumbling noise like the wheels of some vehicle. It drew near; the tramp of horses' feet became distinctly audible, when suddenly it ceased altogether. Five anxious minutes passed; nothing was heard. Lady Emily listened and listened. She began to doubt whether her ears had not deceived her, but now the rustling of the dead leaves foretold an approaching footstep. She knew the tread, none but St Clair had such a stately and martial stride. Forward she darted like an arrow from a bow, and in another instant was clasped to Lord Ronald's bosom. After the first mute greetings were over, he said in a low smothered tone, 'Come, dearest, let us not lose a moment. Silence and dispatch are necessary for our safety.' They accordingly proceeded down the avenue, at the end of which a carriage was awaiting their approach. Into it, Lady Emily was handed by her lover who, as he warmly pressed the hand which had been put into his as she entered the chaise, whispered in the same suppressed voice as before that he would follow her on horseback. 'Very well, my lord,' said Emily, gently returning his grasp. He closed the door, mounted a horse which stood near, gave the word of departure, and soon, by the aid of four wheels and six steeds, the fair runaway left her guardian's castle far behind.

In less than an hour they had rolled over the four miles of road which intervened between them and Verdopolis, passed through the wide streets of that city, now all still and desolate, and entered a great road which ran northward through an extensive forest. After two hours of travelling through the dense gloom of woodland shade, the carriage turned aside from the main path into a byway. They now struck still deeper into the brownish obscurity of oak and palm, elm and cedar. Darkly and dimly, branch rose above branch, each uplifting a thicker canopy of night like foliage, till not a single ray of light could find an opening by which to direct the belated traveller's passing underneath.

At last, to Lady Emily's great satisfaction, the trees began to grow thinner; gradually they assumed a scattered appearance, and ere long the carriage entered an open glade where, standing in the full brilliancy of moonlight, there appeared a lofty and ruinous tower. Wallflowers were waving from its mouldering battlements, and ivy tendrils twined gracefully round the stone mullions of windows from which the glass had long disappeared. Lady Emily shuddered as the carriage stopped before the iron gate of this dreary edifice.

'This will be a dismal hole to sleep in,' said she to herself. 'But why should I be afraid? St Clair is certainly the best judge of the places we ought to halt at.'

The door was now unfastened by a footman who, as the Earl had not yet come up, offered to assist her in getting out of the carriage. When she had descended, the man proceeded to demand entrance. The loud clamorous din which was produced by the agitation of the rusty knocker strangely interrupted that profound and solemn silence which reigned through the primeval forest, while it awoke a hollow echo within the grey desolate ruin. After a long pause the withdrawal of bolts and bars was heard. The portals slowly unfolded and revealed a figure whose appearance was in the most perfect keeping with everything around. It was that of an old woman bent double with the weight of years. Her countenance, all wrinkled and shrivelled, wore a settled expression of discontent, while her small, red eyes gleamed with fiendlike malignity. In one shaking hand she held a huge bunch of rusty keys, and in the other a dimly glittering torch.

'Well, Bertha,' said the footman. 'I have brought you a visitor. You must show her up to the highest chamber for I suppose there's no other in a habitable condition.'

'No. How should there I wonder,' replied the hag, in an angry mumbling tone, 'when nobody's slept in them for more than sixty long years. But what have you brought such a painted toy as this here for? There's no good in the wind, I think.'

'Silence, you old witch!' said the man, 'or I'll cut your tongue out.' Then, addressing Lady Emily, he continued, 'I hope, madam, you'll excuse such an attendant as she is for the present. Had there been time to produce a better, my master would not have failed to do so.'

Lady Emily replied that she could make every allowance for old age, and was proceeding to speak a few kind words to the miserable being, when she turned abruptly away, and muttering, 'Follow me, my fine madam, an you want to see your sleeping-place,' hobbled out of the apartment.

Our heroine immediately complied with her request or rather command, and leaving the roofless hall in which she then stood, followed the hideous crone through a suite of damp empty rooms, through which the wind was sighing in tones too wildly mournful not to communicate a feeling of sympathetic melancholy to the heart of every listener. At length they reached a room smaller than the others, to which a canopy-couch with faded velvet curtains, a few chairs, a table, and an old-fashioned carved wardrobe gave a habitable, if not a comfortable appearance. Here the old woman stopped and, placing the candle on the table, said, 'Now here you may lie till tomorrow if spirits don't run away with you.'

'Oh, I have no fear of that,' replied Lady Emily, forcing a laugh, 'but, my good Bertha, can you not light a fire in that grate, for it's very cold?'

'No, not I,' replied the hag. 'I've something else to do indeed.' And with these ungracious words she walked, or rather crept, out of the room.

When she was gone, Lady Emily very naturally fell into a fit of rather sorrowful musing. The clandestine and secret nature of the past, the dreariness of the present, and the uncertainty of the future, all contributed to impress her mind with the deepest gloom. Ere long, however, the image of St Clair rising like the sun above a threatening horizon, dispelled the sadness which hung over her mind.

'Soon,' thought she, 'he will be here, and then this decayed tower will to me wear the aspect of a king's palace.'

Scarcely had this consoling reflection been uttered in a half-whispered soliloquy when a stately stride and jingling spurs sounded from the antechamber. The door which stood ajar was gently pushed open, and the Earl's tall form, wrapped in a travelling cloak and with a plumed bonnet darkly shading his noble features, appeared at the entrance.

'You are come at last,' said Lady Emily. 'How long you have been! I was almost beginning to fear that you had lost your way in that dismal wood.'

'Beautiful creature,' replied he, in a tone which thrilled through her like an electric shock. 'I would give everything I possess on earth to be in reality an object of such tender interest in your eyes. But, alas, I fear that your sweet sympathy is directed to one who, while I live, shall never more hear it expressed by that silvery voice. Behold me, fair lady, and know into whose power you have fallen!'

So saying, he flung off at once the enshrouding cloak and hat, and there stood before the horror-stricken lady, not the form of her lover, St Clair, but that of his rival, Colonel Percy. The ghastly paleness which instantly overspread her face, and the sudden clasping of her hands, alone proclaimed what feelings passed through her mind as she beheld this unexpected apparition.

'Come, cheer up!' continued the colonel, with a scornful smile. 'It's as well to settle your mind now, for I swear by everything earthly or heavenly, sacred or profane, that this painter-lover of yours – this romancing, arrow-shooting artist –

68

has seen your face for the last time.'

'Wretch!' exclaimed Lady Emily, her eyes sparkling with scorn and hatred. 'Know that he whom you call my painter-lover has higher and purer blood in his veins than you. He is Earl St Clair of Clan Albyn, and you are but the dependent hanger-on of a noble relative.'

'So he has told you,' returned Percy. 'But, damsel, be he lord or limner, I have fairly outwitted him this time. His chariot wheels tarried somewhat too long, methinks. Mine were better oiled – they ran smoother. I won the race and have borne off the prize triumphantly. He may now cry "St Clair to the rescue!" but none of his plaided minions can reach the length of this dark and unknown retreat.'

'Unprincipled villain!' said Lady Emily, whose high spirit was now fully roused. 'You have acted treacherously, you have adopted means totally unbecoming the honour of a gentleman, or never should I have been thus ensnared by your toils.'

'Humph,' replied the colonel. 'I am not one of those punctilious fools who consider honour as the god of their idolatry. Eavesdroppers, spies, or false witnesses are all equally acceptable to me when there is a great end in view which can be more easily obtained by their assistance.'

'Colonel Percy,' said Lady Emily, 'for I can call you by no name so detestable as your own, do you intend to keep me in this tower or to send me back to Clydesdale Castle?'

'I shall keep you here most assuredly till you promise to become my wife, and then you shall reappear in Verdopolis with a magnificence suitable to the future Duchess of Beaufort.'

'Then here I remain till death or some happier chance relieves me, for not all the tortures that man's ingenuity could devise should ever induce me to marry one whose vices have sunk him so low in the ranks of humanity as yours have, one who openly renounces the dominion of honour, and declares that he has given himself up to the blind guidance of his own departed inclinations.'

'Excellently well preached!' remarked the colonel, with a sneer. 'But, fair worshipper of honour, this resolution will not prevent the proposed incarceration which shall be inflicted on you as a sort of punishment for having flagrantly violated the decrees of that deity whose cause you so eloquently advocate. Pray, my lady, was it quite consistent with the dictates of honour to deceive your old doting uncle, and elope at midnight with an unknown adventurer?'

This taunt was too much for Lady Emily. The remembrance of her uncle, and of what his sufferings would be when her disappearance should be known, instantly destroyed that semblance of dignity which pride had taught her to assume in order to overawe her suitor's familiar insolence. She leant her head on her hand and burst into a flood of bitter tears.

'Those crystal drops,' said the colonel, totally unmoved by her distress, 'tell me that it would be no very difficult matter to soften your apparently stubborn heart. Could I but remain here one day longer, I am certain that the powers of persuasion I possess would succeed in bringing my Queen of Beauty to reason, but unfortunately dire necessity commands my immediate departure. Before sunrise I ought to be in Verdopolis, and day is already breaking over those eastern hills. Farewell,' he continued, in a more serious tone. 'Farewell Lady Emily, I am going where there is likely to be hot work and perhaps some black rebel's sabre may before long rid you of a sincere, though rejected lover, and the world of what most men call a villain.'

'Farewell, colonel,' replied his weeping captive. 'And remember that if such should be your fate, the recollection of what you have this night done will not tend to alleviate the agonies of death.'

'Pshaw!' said he, with a reckless laugh. 'Do you think I have any fears on that score? No, my conscience – if I ever had any – has been long seared. Immortality finds no place in my creed, and death is with me but an abbreviated term for lasting sleep. Once more farewell.'

With these words he snatched her hand, kissed it fervently, and departed. The twilight glimmer of dawn was now stealing through the narrow casements of Lady Emily's prison and, falling on her face and person as she lay stretched on the tattered velvet couch where, overcome with fatigue, she had now thrown herself, revealed a touching picture of Beauty in Distress. Her hair hung in loose and neglected curls on her snowy neck and shoulder, her eyes were closed, her long dark lashes, wet with tears, rested motionless on her cheek except when a fresh drop trembled on their silken fringes. Her face, usually blooming, was now pale as alabaster from the misery of the sleepless night she had passed. One white hand and arm supported her head on the pillow, and the other confined the folds of the dark mantle in which she was partially enveloped.

After some time – in spite of the wretchedness of her situation, separated, it might be for ever, from all she held dear on earth, and confined in a solitary ruin with no other attendant than the withered hag Bertha – she fell into a deep slumber, and while she enjoys this temporary respite from affliction, we will revert to other matters.

## 6

It is well known that the great war between the Ashantees and Twelves ended, after their many bloody and obstinate battles, in the complete subjugation of the former; their prince being slain, their nation nearly annihilated, their metropolis destroyed and the circumjacent country reduced to a condition of the wildest and most appalling desolation which the imagination of man can conceive. Quashie, the King's only son, then at the tender age of four or five years, was taken prisoner. At the general partition of booty, he, with other captives, fell to the share of His Grace the Duke of Wellington, from whom he experienced as much care and tenderness as if he had been the monarch's son instead of his slave.

In these guilded fetters the young prince grew up. His literary education was duly cared for, but he declined to profit by the instructions bestowed on him further than as it regarded the acquisition of the English and Ashantee languages, and the capability of expressing himself in both by pen as well as tongue. In bodily exercises and military affairs, however, the case was different. Everything relating to these he learnt with an avidity which showed how fully he inherited his father's warlike spirit. At the age of seventeen, he was a tall, handsome youth, black as jet and with an eye full of expression and fire. His disposition was bold, irritable, active, daring and at the same time deeply treacherous.

It now began to appear that, notwithstanding the care with which he had been treated by his conquerors, he retained against them, as if by instinct, the most deeply rooted and inveterate hatred. Since his fifteenth year he had been accustomed to take long excursions by himself among the mountains and forests of Ashantee for the purpose, as he said, of hunting the wild animals that abound there. But sub-sequent events showed that his real employment during these expeditions was discovering and prompting to rebellion the hidden tribes of Africans who, after the destruction of Coomassie and the slaughter of King Quamina, had concealed themselves in fastnesses inaccessible to any but a native of the country. When he had sufficiently kindled in these wild savages a spirit of slumbering discontent, and roused them to make an effort for regaining that independence as a nation which they had lost, he, in conjunction with the celebrated brothers Budi and Benini, formerly his father's favourite counsellors, unfurled the royal standard of Ashantee and summoned the scattered remnant of that once mighty empire to join him without delay at the foot of Mount Pindus.

It seemed as if this invocation had called from their graves a portion of the vast army which fourteen years since had reddened with their blood the lofty heights of Rosendale Hill. Multitudes flocked to his banner from the mountain glens and caverns of Jibbel Kumri, from the unexpected regions of inner Africa, and from the almost boundless desert of Sahara, so that in a few weeks no less than fifteen thousand armed natives of a kingdom which was supposed to have been extirpated, declared themselves ready to shed the last drop of their blood in vindication of Quashie II's claim to his ancestral throne.

With this determination they marched towards Verdopolis and had arrived within four hundred miles of that city before intelligence of what had taken place reached the Twelves. When the fact of this rebellion was known, however, the Duke of Wellington immediately desired that the punishment of the rebels might be left to him, as the young viper who commanded them had been nourished on his own hearth and brought up by him with almost parental tenderness. His request was immediately granted, and the Duke dispatched ten thousand troops under the command of General Leaf, a descendant, by the way, of the famous Captain Leaf, to stop the progress of the insurgents.

When Quashie heard of the formidable force which was advancing against him, he sent an ambassador to Gondar, requesting assistance from the Abyssinian King and, in the meantime, commenced a very orderly retreat. Ras Michael, who detested the British, readily permitted an army of eight thousand soldiers to assist Quashie in his bold enterprise against them. With this reinforcement the young warrior ventured to give the enemy battle. An engagement accordingly ensued near Fateconda on the Senegal, which, after a very obstinate contest, ended rather in favour of the Verdopolitans, though the victory they gained was of the nature that another similar one would have been total destruction.

A fresh addition now arrived from Abyssinia so that the army of the rebels was very little the worse for their defeat, while Leaf's force amounted barely to six thousand men. The Duke, being informed of this state of things, immediately ordered out sixteen regiments and, placing himself at their head, marched without delay to the scene of the action. On his arrival he found that the enemy had been joined by a large body of Moors from the north so that he was still far inferior in numbers, but trusting to the superior discipline of his troops, he determined to stand his ground without further reinforcement.

Having given the reader this necessary information I will now proceed with my narrative in a more detailed and less historical style.

It was a glorious evening in the end of summer when the hostile armies lay encamped on opposite banks of the River

Senegal. The sun was slowly approaching the horizon of a speckless sky, and threw his parting rays with softened brilliancy over a scene of unsurpassed loveliness. Between the two hosts lay a beautiful valley where groves of delicate-leaved tamarind trees and tall palmyras sweetly shadowed the blue bright waters of the wandering stream. A cluster of deserted huts, whose inhabitants had fled at the approach of soldiers, crowned the gently sloped acclivity which embosomed the glen. On one side, in the largest of these, the Duke of Wellington had taken up his quarters, and here he now sat surrounded by four of his principal officers. Two of these are already known to our readers, being the Marquis of Charlesworth and Colonel Percy. Of the remaining two, the first was a middle-sized man with broad shoulders and spindle shanks. His forehead was rather high, his nose large and projecting, his mouth wide, and his chin remarkably long; he was dressed in uniform with a star on his breast and large cambric ruffles at each wrist. The other was a little personage with jointless limbs, a chubby face, and a pale pink wig of frazzled silk surmounted by a tall black hat on which was an ornament of carved wood.

These officers were conversing with each other in undertones not to disturb the Duke's meditations, who sat with his eyes fixed on the wide prospect which opened before him, and which was bounded by a dim sweeping milk-white line indicating the commencement of the great sandy desert.

'Bobadil,' said he, suddenly addressing himself to the former of the two gentlemen I have just described. 'Do you not perceive something moving in the direction of the enemy's camp? It is under the shadow of that lofty hill to the north and appears like a dark and compact body of men. Surely it is not some new ally?'

Bobadil came forward and began to poke out his neck, strain and wink his eyes, look through his fingers etc., but finally declared he could perceive nothing. The Marquis of Charlesworth and General Leaf, the owner of the pink wig, were equally unsuccessful.

'You are a set of moles,' said the Duke. 'I see them most distinctly – they have rounded the hill and their arms are glittering brightly in the sunshine. Come hither, Percy, can't you see that flashing hedge of spears with a banner displayed in the rear?'

'Certainly, my lord,' replied Percy, whose younger eyes could easily discern what was quite lost to the dimmed optics of the old generals. 'They are now turned from the rebels and seem advancing towards us.'

A silence of a quarter of an hour here ensued, during which the Duke continued to gaze intently at the approaching army, for such it was now distinctly seen to be. They slowly wound away from the Ashantee camp and, entering a deep valley, were for the present lost to sight. But ere long a burst of wild music heralded their reappearance. Gradually they emerged from the sinuous winding of the glen which had concealed them, and in martial array advanced to the sound of shrill pipes and deep-toned kettledrums along the right bank of the Senegal.

'Those are not foes but friends,' exclaimed the Duke, starting up. 'Upon my word, St Clair has kept his promise well! I did not think his northern hills could send forth such a fine body of troops.'

'Who are they, my lord?' exclaimed all the officers at once, with the exception of Percy, whose brow had suddenly grown dark at the mention of St Clair.

'The men of Elimbos, the lads of the mist,' replied His Grace. 'Here, Percy, order my horse and your own and attend me whilst I go to meet them.'

Percy left the hut and in a few minutes the Duke and himself were galloping down towards the valley. As they drew near that Highland host my father frequently expressed his admiration at the perfect order in which the ranks moved, the athletic appearance and uncommon stature of the men who formed them, and the clean, well-burnished appearance of their arms and equipment. Just as they reached the advanced guard, a general halt was called, both rode through the unfolding columns till, on gaining the centre of the little army, they perceived the Earl, surrounded by his choicest vassals, all dressed in the green tartan of their clan, and bearing spears, bows, quivers, and small triangular shields. Near him stood a gigantic warrior whose snow-white hair and beard proclaimed advanced age, while from his erect bearing and Herculean frame and sinewy limbs it was easy to perceive that he retained unimpaired all the vigorous powers of youth. He bore in one hand a huge spear proportionate to his own titanic size, from which floated the broad folds of a green banner bearing as a device a golden eagle with expanded wings and the motto: 'I dwell on the rock.' This person was the celebrated Donald of the Standard, called, in common parlance, 'the ape of the hills'. He is now one hundred and ten years of age, and consequently was, at that period, ninety. After a cordial greeting on each side, the Duke proceeded to direct St Clair how to encamp his men and to give him other instructions which it is unnecessary here to recapitulate. Their conference being ended, he took leave for the night and returned with Colonel Percy to his own quarters.

It may now be as well to connect the broken thread of my rambling narrative before I proceed further.

When St Clair reached Verdopolis after his interview with Lady Emily Charlesworth at Clydesdale Castle, he ordered his page to go to the nearest place where carriages were let out to hire and order one to be in readiness by eleven o'clock that night. From some unexplained cause of delay it was not prepared till past twelve, and consequently the bird was flown before he arrived at the appointed place of rendezvous. In a state of impatience amounting almost to madness, he continued to pace the chestnut avenue, watching the setting of the moon, the slow vanishing of the stars, and the gradual approach of daylight, listening to every breath of wind and transforming the rustle of each falling leaf into the step of his expected fair one. Morning broke, however, the sun rose, the deer awoke from their light slumbers, and still Lady Emily came not.

Stung to the heart with her apparent infidelity, he determined to learn the cause of it from her own mouth, and if a satisfactory excuse were not assigned, to bid her an eternal farewell; with this resolution he hastened to the castle. On his arrival he found it all in confusion, the servants hurrying to and fro with countenances of doubt and dismay. On enquiring the reason of this unusual movement, he was informed that Lady Emily had disappeared that night and that no one knew where she was gone. Terror-struck at this intelligence, he immediately returned to Verdopolis where he remained for some days, during which time the most diligent research was made after the unfortunate lady by her afflicted uncle, but all to no purpose. Finding this to be the case, St Clair, who had now lost all motive for desiring a continuance of life and whose bitter and heart-gnawing anguish rendered a quiescent state of existence the most terrible of all others, determined immediately to offer his own services and those of his clan, whose chieftain he was, to the Duke of Wellington in his intended expedition against the Ashantees. This proposal, of course, was gratefully accepted, and St Clair soon after departed to gather his warriors and lead them from their native mountains. With his opportune arrival the reader is already acquainted and now, having cleared scores, I may trot on unencumbered.

On the evening of the day which followed that event, the Earl sat in his tent with no other companion than the little page Andrew who, squatting like a Turk in one corner, was employed in burnishing his master's spear and silver quiver. Colonel Percy rode up on his gallant warhorse and informed St Clair that the Duke was about to hold a council of war in which his presence would be required. It was with difficulty that our hero managed to return a civil answer to the unwelcome envoy. With a haughtiness of gesture and a sternness of tone that ill-suited the courteous nature of the words, he replied that he felt highly flattered by the Duke's request and would attend him without delay. Whether Percy experienced any reciprocation of animosity I know not, but his countenance expressed none as, with a bland smile and low inclination of the head, he touched his horse's sides and caracoled gaily away.

The council was held in a large tent covered with scarlet cloth, richly ornamented with gold embroidery, and from the summit waved a crimson flag bearing the arms of England. When St Clair entered this superb pavilion, he found the Duke surrounded by about twenty officers. At his left hand sat the Marquis of Charlesworth whose pale countenance and abstracted air told a melancholy tale of recent affliction. The Earl was invited by His Grace to take the seat at his right hand which was vacant. At this flattering mark of distinction Colonel Percy, who sat near the entrance of the tent among the junior officers, was observed to smile with a peculiar expression.

'Now gentlemen,' said the Duke, when all were assembled. 'I do not intend to detain you for long. My motive for assembling you together was merely to obtain your approbation of a proposal for settling our Black friends on the other side of the river in a few hours, without, I trust, incurring much risk to our own army.'

His Grace then proceeded to unfold a scheme for attacking the enemy's camp at night when they would be wholly unable to make any adequate defence, it having been ascertained by means of spies that their watch was not one of the most vigilant in the world. The advantage of this plan being obvious, the council gave a unanimous opinion in its favour, and the next night was assigned as the period for putting it into execution.

Business being thus summarily disposed of, the Duke proceeded to say: 'Since, gentlemen, I have called you together for an affair of such brevity, some reparation is due. I hope therefore you will not refuse to partake with me of a soldier's supper. It is prepared and now only waits your approach.' As he spoke, the curtain at the upper end of the tent was withdrawn and revealed an inner pavilion, brilliantly lit, in which was a long table covered with the material for an excellent and substantial, though not perhaps luxurious supper. All willingly accepted the invitation except the Marquis of Charlesworth, who pleaded an inability to enjoy festivity as an excuse for declining it.

'I will not press you, my lord,' said the Duke kindly, taking his hand, 'but remember that solitude nourishes grief.'

The old man's only reply was a mournful shake of the head.

'That poor fellow has had a heavy stroke in his old age,' observed Colonel Percy, who happened to be seated next to St Clair at supper. 'He has lost a very pretty and accomplished niece in a most unaccountable manner.'

'Has he?' said the Earl, eyeing his neighbour with a glance that might have struck terror to the heart of a lion.

'Yes,' pursued the colonel, in a tone of the most provoking calmness. 'Ah! she was a sweet girl, rather capricious, though, as most women are. One of her fancies was particularly absurd.'

'What might that be?' asked St Clair.

'Why, you'll hardly believe it when I tell you. She took it into her head to fall in love with a poor, silly, sneaking puppy of a painter, and for some time declared she would marry him in preference to the nephew and heir of a duke. But at length the latter lover prevailed, and then the little witch confessed she had only been playing the coquette to try her suitor's fidelity and that, in reality, she despised the man of canvas as much as she did the meanest of his signpost daubs.'

The flush which crimsoned St Clair's cheek and brow, and the light which sparkled in his fierce eyes would have quelled the insolence of an ordinary man, but they only increased that of the demi-fiend who sat by, rejoicing in his agony.

'You are not subject to apoplectic fits are you, sir?' said he, gazing on him with affected wonder.

'No,' replied the Earl, suppressing his wrath by a strong effort. 'But, sir, how will the successful lover bear the loss of his intended bride?'

'Oh, they say he displays a laudable degree of resignation under the affliction.'

'Then his affliction for her was a pretence?'

'No, I don't say that; but you know, my lord, he is perhaps better acquainted with her whereabouts than other people. Hum, don't you understand me?'

'Indeed I do not.'

'Why then, to speak more plainly, some folks don't hesitate to say that she has eloped.'

'Sir,' said the Earl in a low deep voice, 'let me tell you I am in some degree acquainted with the parties we have been conversing about, and let me tell you further that if I were her uncle and entertained the least suspicion of the kind you hint at, I would cause the infernal scoundrel, her lover, to be torn limb from limb by wild horses, or force him to tell me where the unhappy creature is concealed.'

'Ha! Would you?' said the colonel, while a cloud at once fell on his brow, and he instinctively grasped the weapon at his side. But almost directly after, he muttered, 'the hour is not yet arrived,' and his countenance resumed its former state of deceitful composure.

The dishes were now removed and wine was introduced. After the first few rounds the Duke of Wellington, rising from his seat at the head of the table, begged to be excused from a longer stay at the festive board. He then drank to the health of all his guests, and bidding them goodnight withdrew. St Clair, who was in no mood for joining in the riotous mirth that now became the principal characteristic of the military mess, took the first opportunity of following his example.

The night was still and calm, its dewy coolness and the mild moonlight which was poured down upon him at intervals as he wandered among the silent tents and through the dark groves, which waved with scarce visible motion along the river's shelving banks, served in a great measure to soothe his roused and exaggerated passions. But not all the deep tranquillity which fell like balm from the blue starry sky, not all the images of rest and serenity which a sweet summer's night ever creates could bring corresponding peace to his love-tortured heart, or expel the worm of jealousy that now gnawed his very vitals. To be despised by her for whom he could have given his lifeblood, to be the object of her derision and scorn, to have all his suspicions of her good faith so fearfully verified, was worse than death to his proud haughty spirit.

As he stood on the river's brink and looked down on the deep clear waters which flowed so gently and wooingly at his feet, he longed to cool the delirium of his brain by a spring into their liquid freshness. Putting aside, however, this suggestion of the tempter, and half despising himself for being so moved by the false-heartedness of a fickle woman, he turned from the stream and proceeded towards his own tent. Just as he was about to enter it, a voice whispered in his ear: 'Beware of Percy, it is a friend who warns you.'

The Earl looked hastily round; he saw a dark figure gliding away which was soon lost in the shadow of a lofty cluster of palm trees.

For a long time after he had lain himself on his deer-skin couch that night, slumber refused to visit his aching eyelids. The warning of his unknown friend joined to the other subjects of deep and intense thought which filled his distracted mind, for some hours effectually banished sleep from his pillow. But at last wearied nature, being quite worn out, was compelled to seek refuge in temporary repose. Scarcely had kindly oblivion fallen over the sorrows which oppressed him when a long and peculiarly shrill whistle sounded without the tent. Andrew, who till this moment had been apparently fast asleep in a corner, now softly and cautiously left his couch and, taking a small lamp, stepped on tiptoe to his master's bedside. Having ascertained that he really was slumbering by holding the light to his closed eyes, the page wrapped himself in a green plaid and, without noise, left the tent. At the outside a man was standing whose blue coat and liveried hat showed him to be the same person that had abducted Andrew about a month since. Without word spoken, both walked, or rather stole away towards a neighbouring grove, the footman leading the way and beckoning Andrew to follow. Here they were joined by another figure in a cloak. All three then proceeded down the river, and in a few minutes the intervening trees entirely concealed them from view.

## 7

'Well, my lord, the day is ours at last, but we've had a hard tug for the victory. Upon my word, those Black rascals fought like devils!'

'They did indeed, and I think their overthrow, considering all the circumstances of the case, may be accounted almost a miracle.'

'Truly it may. By the by, St Clair, I shall hold a second council of war this evening. Those circumstances you allude to require explanation. They must be carefully looked into – you will attend of course?'

'Certainly, my lord.'

Such was the brief dialogue between St Clair and the Duke of Wellington as the latter rode by with his staff. A bloody but decisive victory had just been gained over the Ashantee, though in a manner different from what had been at first intended.

At eleven o'clock of the night appointed for the secret attack, the Duke of Wellington crossed the Senegal at the head of his whole army. As they drew near the hostile camp, not a voice whispered, not a light glimmered among the long, silent rows of snow-white tents. Unopposed, they held on their course to Quashie's own pavilion. They entered – it was empty. A short space of time sufficed to ascertain that not a living thing save themselves remained in all the deserted camp. Those who were near the Duke when this discovery was made said that for a few moments his countenance expressed a depth of disappointment akin to despair. He recovered himself, however, almost directly, and ordered scouts to disperse instantly in every direction and find out which way the enemy was gone. Ere long some of them returned with the information that they had marched northwards and were now halting about ten miles off. The army immediately received orders to take the route indicated, which led up the valley.

About daybreak they arrived at a wild mountain pass, through which might be seen a vast plain where the allied forces of the Moors, Ashantees and Abyssinians, were all drawn up in battle array. It was a gorgeous but terrific spectacle as the first sunbeams flashed on that dusky host, and lit up to fiercer radiance their bright weapons and all the barbarous magnificence of gold and gems in which most of the warriors were attired. As the Duke's army, with himself at their head, filed slowly forward through the narrow gorge, a young horseman sped suddenly to the front of the African array and, waving his long lance in the air, exclaimed, 'Freedom would this night have received her death stab from the hand of the White Tyrant had not a traitor arisen in the camp of oppression.' With these words he plunged again into the ranks and disappeared, but not before the golden diadem glittering on his forehead had revealed the arch-rebel, Quashie.

The contest which then ensued, and which dyed the plains of Camalia with blood, I need not describe: it is a matter of history. Suffice it to say that of the twenty-five thousand gallant rebels whom the sun's rising rays had that morning lit to the contest, high in hope and strong in valour, the bodies of seventeen thousand eight hundred, ere evening, lay cold and still on a lost field of battle, waiting till the vultures of Jibbel Kumri should scent the banquet from afar, and grant them a living sepulchre in their devouring maws.

Our hero St Clair had played one of the most conspicuous parts in the day's tragedy. Reckless of life, which was now hateful to him, he sought glory at the head of his brave highlanders wherever the fight raged thickest, and almost wished that the renown his dauntless courage was certain to earn might ring through the world whilst he himself lay in the voiceless tomb, shrouded in his last garments and hushed to repose in the slumber from which none can awake.

Fate, however, had decreed otherwise. The scimitar of the turbaned moor, the war-spear of the savage Ashantee, and even the renowned arrow of the quivered Abyssinian seemed all to have lost their powers of destruction when turned against him; and when the battle was past and he, with his little army, slowly retraced their steps over the gory plain, it was with feelings approaching to envy that he viewed the ghastly corpses which, pale and mangled, lay scattered around.

On arriving at his own tent, he called Andrew to assist him in changing his soiled and bloody dress, the page however did not obey this summons, and after waiting some time in expectation of his appearance, he was obliged to manage as well as he could without any aid, Having completed his toilet and partaken of some refreshment, he hastened, as it was now late, to attend the council.

A profound silence pervaded the pavilion as he entered, broken only by an occasional whisper. The Duke was sitting at the head of the table in an unusually pensive and meditative posture, his head resting on his hand, his brows contracted, and an expression of deep solemnity diffused over his whole countenance. When St Clair was seated, he looked up and glanced quickly round, as if to ascertain that all the members were assembled, then rising, he proceeded to address them briefly thus:

'Gentlemen, the cause for which you are convened this night is of the last importance. It is to make an enquiry which will involve the life and honour of some individual or individuals amongst you. Two days ago, a plan was broached in this place for attacking our enemies by night: they obtained intelligence of it, and it was frustrated. Our business is now to discover how that intelligence reached them. I grieve to say that the words which you have all heard the rebel-leader utter this day in the face of both armies have raised the horrible suspicion in my mind that it was by treachery. The traitor must be in this apartment, and if he will now confess his guilt, I solemnly promise to spare his life, but if he leaves it to be found out by another, then a death the most painful and dishonourable shall be his.'

The Duke ceased. His stern and keen eye scrutinised the countenances of all who surrounded him, one by one, as if he would, by that means, have read the thoughts passing in every heart.

For some minutes not a word was spoken; each regarded his neighbour with a visage in which awe, curiosity and aimless suspicion were strangely mingled. The dim torchlight of the pavilion, however, showed one person whose calm and noble features displayed none of these emotions but, on the contrary, something like a lurking smile played around the corners of his mouth. It was Colonel Percy.

In a short time he rose and, advancing to the table where the Duke sat, said in a low voice, 'Will Your Grace permit me to speak?'

'Certainly,' was the reply.

'Then,' continued the colonel, drawing his tall form up to the fullness of its majestic height, and coolly folding his arms, 'I have it in my power to reveal the wretch who betrayed his general and his comrades, but before I mention the craven's name, he shall have one more opportunity of saving his worthless life. Conscience-stricken traitor, step forward and avail yourself of that mercy which is even now passing away never to return.'

A breathless pause followed this awful appeal; not a whisper sounded, not a foot or hand moved.

'You will not accept the offered boon?' said Percy, in deep thrilling tones. 'Then your blood be upon your own head. My lord,' he went on, turning to the Duke, while a supernatural light rose in his triumphant glance, 'know that the base traitor sits at your right hand. Yes, the most noble Ronald, Lord of St Clair, and Chieftain of Clan Albyn, has been bribed by the Negro's wealth to blot with treachery a scutcheon owned by a hundred earls.'

One universal exclamation of 'Impossible!' broke forth at this strange accusation. Each member of the council started from his seat, and an expression of astonishment, amounting almost to horror, appeared in every countenance. The Duke and St Clair alone sat unmoved.

'Sir,' said the former, calmly and somewhat sternly, 'the most ample proof of this bold charge must be furnished, or that punishment intended for the accused shall recoil upon the accuser.'

'I accept Your Grace's alternative,' replied the colonel, bowing low. 'Testimony is not wanting, but first let me ask His Lordship if he denies the charge.'

'No,' replied the Earl, in a tone of startling vehemence, while he sprung from his seat as if actuated by some overmastering impulse. 'No, I scorn to deny the hellish falsehood, but I will prove its baseness on that tool of Satan with my sword.' As he spoke he snatched the weapon from its scabbard.

'Gentlemen,' said Percy, wholly undisturbed by this action, 'that sword condemns him. Mark it well and then tell me if such a one ought to be in the hands of a British soldier.'

All eyes turned on the glittering blade – it was a curved Moorish scimitar, the handle richly decorated with gems of the highest value.

'That certainly has not been purchased in Verdopolis, my lord,' said the Duke, after examining it. 'How did you obtain it?'

'I know not,' replied St Clair, regarding the weapon with evident surprise. 'It is not my own – I never saw it till this moment.'

'Recollect yourself,' continued his friendly judge. 'Did you take it up by mistake on the field of battle?'

The Earl shook his head.

'Perhaps,' observed Colonel Percy with a sneer, 'I could inform His Lordship how it came into his possession, if Your Grace will allow me to produce my witness.'

The Duke signified his assent, and Percy, advancing towards the tent door, called out, 'Travers, bring in the prisoner.' This summons was answered by the appearance of a footman leading a boy whose keen eye and shrivelled, ill-favoured features instantly proclaimed him to be none other than our friend Andrew.

'How is this?' exclaimed St Clair, stepping back in amazement. 'Why is that boy in your custody? I claim him as my vassal and, as his liege lord, have a right to know of what he is accused.'

'He shall inform you himself, my lord,' said the colonel, significantly.

'No,' interposed the Duke. 'I should like to hear it from you, sir, in the first place.'

'I found him, my lord,' returned Percy, 'beyond the proscribed boundaries of the camp early yesterday morning when I was going my rounds as officer of the watch. On questioning him where he had been, he appeared much agitated and returned no answers but such as were inconsistent and evidently false. I then threatened to punish him severely if he did not speak the truth. This had the desired effect – he immediately confessed that he had been to the African tents. Further questions extorted from him the information on which I have grounded my charge against his master, and which he is now ready to communicate to Your Grace.'

'Andrew,' said the Duke, 'come here. Will you promise to answer me truly such questions as I shall now ask?'

'I will,' said the boy, laying his hand on his heart with great apparent sincerity.

'By whom, then, were you sent to the Ashantee camp?'

'By my lord, the chief.'

'What for?'

'To deliver a paper which was sealed and directed to Quashie II, King of the Liberated Africans.'

'Had you ever been there before?'

'Yes, once.'

'When?'

'That same night.'

'And why did you go then?'

'I was sent to ask for a certain reward which Quashie had promised my master some time before in case he would tell him of all that passed in such councils as he should attend.'

'Did you hear that promise made?'

'Yes.'

'At what time?'

'The first night after we arrived here a Black man came to my lord's tent and offered him twelve ackees (I think he called it) of rock gold if he would do as he wanted him.'

'And your master consented?'

'Yes.'

'Did you see Quashie when you went to his camp?'

'Yes.'

'What was he like?'

'He was a young man and very tall. His nose and lips were not flat and thick like the other Blacks, and he spoke English.'

'The description you have given is very correct. Now tell me what the reward was you carried to your master?'

'There was a black box filled with something very heavy, a large mantle made of different coloured silk, and a sword which Quashie took from his own belt.'

'Describe the sword.'

'It was crooked, almost like a sickle, and had a great many precious stones about the handle.'

Here a general murmur of surprise broke from the bystanders. The Duke, however, sternly rebuked them, and went on: 'Do you know where the black box and silk mantle were put?'

'Yes, my master commanded me to dig a hole in the centre of the tent and bury them there.'

'Bobadil,' said His Grace, 'take one or two men with you to the Earl's tent and see if you can find these articles.'

Bobadil made a deep and silent reverence, and departed to execute his commission. General Leaf now advanced to the table.

'May I ausk,' said he, addressing the page in a tone which retained something of the ancient long-drawn twang, 'whather you were by yourself when you went to the Raubels?'

'No, my master went part of the way with me the first time,' replied Andrew.

'I thought so, for the night before last when I was returning from de counshel saupper, I saw a tall man and a little boy going towards the camp boundaries, and the man was dressed in green plaid such as Laurd St Clair wears.'

'That is conclusive evidence,' observed Colonel Percy.

'It's corroborative,' said the Duke, 'but I do not allow it to be quite conclusive.'

Steps were now heard approaching the door of the pavilion, and in another moment General Bobadil entered, bearing a black box in one hand, and a folded silk garment in the other. He silently deposited both on the table. The Duke first examined the latter article, it was one of those splendid Ashantee cloths which exhibit in their ever-varying hues all the vivid colours of the rainbow. He then opened the casket and took out its contents, which consisted of five double gold chains, each two yards long, a collar and a pair of bracelets of the same costly metal, several ornaments in aggry beads, and an amulet in a gold case, blazing with the finest diamonds.

'Good God!' said he, when he had completed the survey. 'I could not have thought that these paltry trinkets would have purchased a British soldier's faith. St Clair, rise – let me hear your defence. I wish with my whole heart that you may be able to disprove all we have heard this night.'

'My lord,' said the Earl, who had hitherto been sitting motionless with his head muffled in his plaid. 'I have no defence to make. Heaven knows my innocence, but how can I prove to man that all the seemingly fair and consistent evidence which has just been delivered is in reality a most Satanic compound of the deepest and blackest falsehoods. My destiny is at present dark and gloomy. I will wait with patience till a better prospect rises.'

So saying, he folded his arms, and resumed his former

attitude. The Duke then proceeded to say that he should not yet pass sentence, but should give the accused six weeks to collect witnesses and prepare for a formal trial. He informed him likewise that he should be instantly conveyed to Verdopolis and intimated his intention of repairing thither himself as soon as the rebellion should be finally quelled. The council now broke up and St Clair was removed by a band of soldiers to the tent usually appropriated to prisoners.

I must beg the reader to imagine that a space of six weeks has elapsed before he again beholds my hero, during which time he has been removed to Verdopolis and placed in one of those state dungeons that lie under the Tower of All Nations.

It was a gloomy place, a thousand feet below the upper world. The thick walls and the low roof, elevated on short broad arches as massive as the rock whence they were hewn, admitted no sound, however faint, transient and far away, by which the tenant of this living tomb might be reminded that near three million of his fellow men were living and moving in the free light of heaven above him. The dead, the dreary silence which hung in the grave-like atmosphere was, however, broken at intervals by a noise which, low indeed and seemingly as distant as the earth's central abyss, yet shook the dungeon's walls, and as it reverberated among the other subterranean caverns which were excavated above, below and around, rung on the ear with a deep hollow boom that chilled the heart and brought the sweat-drops of terror to the brow. This was the clam-clam sounding through the underground passages, a thousand miles in length from the haunted hills of Jibbel Kumri.

Here on the evening of the day preceding the one appointed for his final trial, St Clair lay stretched on a bed of straw.

A glimmering lamp was placed on the damp ground beside him, its feeble rays inadequate to dissipate the almost palpable darkness which shrouded the remote recesses of this fearful prison, yet shed a faint dying light on the unfortunate nobleman's wasted person and features. Not a trace remained of that bright bloom which health and youthful vigour had once communicated to his now wan and sunken cheek. The light of his eye, however, yet remained unquenched; the princely beauty of his countenance, though faded, was not destroyed.

Suddenly, as a harsh, grating sound like a key turning in a rusty lock proclaimed the gaoler's approach, he started from his recumbent position and sat upright. It was full ten minutes before all the fastenings which secured the dungeon door were removed, but at length the last bolt was withdrawn, and the heavy iron portals being unfolded, gave admittance not to the gaoler, but to a tall man whose form and face were wholly concealed by the foldings of his ample mantle. With a slow and cautious step he advanced towards the Earl's straw couch, and placing himself on that side which was most dimly illumi nated by the lamp, addressed him thus: 'Earl of St Clair, if I mistake not, you lie here on the charge of Treachery.'

'And if I do,' replied the prisoner, whose spirit confinement had not in the least subdued, 'does that circumstance give strangers a right to insult me by the mention of it?'

'Certainly not,' returned the unknown visitor, unmoved by the indirect reproach which his words conveyed. 'Nor did I intend to insult you by the question I have just asked. My firm conviction is that you are innocent of the crime laid to your charge – do I err in that belief?'

'Do you err in a belief of your own existence?'

'I should think not.'

'Be as certain, then, of the one fact as you are of the other and you will be right.'

'That is decisive,' replied the stranger, in a tone which revealed that a smile was curling his lip; and then, after a pause, he added, 'My lord, does not your trial for this false offence come on tomorrow?'

'It does.'

'And are you provided with evidence to disprove it?'

'No, and I doubt not that before forty-eight hours go by, I shall have fallen a victim to the hate of a malignant enemy. Yes, the last son of the Lords of Roslyn will go to his grave branded with the name of traitor.'

'Not if I can help it!' said the unknown. 'And I will do my utmost.'

'Stranger, you are kind, but what, alas! is it in your power to effect? The evidence against me is strong, the web of deceit has been woven with impenetrable art.'

'Oh, but fear nothing. Truth shall prevail at last. Tell me only who your concealed enemy is.'

'Colonel Percy, my accuser.'

'I thought as much, and now I come to the object of my visit to you in this loathsome dungeon: why does he hate you?'

'Before I answer that question, I must know who it is that asks me.'

'That cannot be,' replied the stranger, drawing his ample cloak more firmly round him. 'Thus far, however, I may say: I am the person who sometime since warned you to beware of Colonel Percy. I was present when the charge was brought against you, and, as I know something of the accuser's character and disposition, I was led to suspect the truth of what he said, knowing that nothing but a motive of the most powerful kind could induce him to be so active in an affair of that nature. I ask you to inform me what this motive is. If you will be candid with me the young vulture shall miss his prey this time.'

'Sir,' replied the Earl, 'there is something in your voice which tells me I ought to trust you. Know then that I loved a woman who, as I thought, was the most beautiful and excellent of her sex. The colonel was my rival and –'

'You have said enough,' interrupted the stranger. 'I need no more to convince me fully of your perfect innocence. In such a case I know Colonel Percy would never rest till he had wreaked on his rival the deepest and deadliest revenge, were that rival his own brother. The whole black conspiracy is now revealed: he is the traitor and, Heaven willing, he shall die the traitor's death. Tomorrow when you are called upon to produce evidence of your innocence, do not hesitate to say that there is one in the court who, if he will, can prove you guiltless of the crime. Leave the rest to me, and now farewell. I hope tomorrow night you will lay your head on a different pillow.'

'Farewell,' said St Clair, warmly grasping the stranger's hand, 'and doubt not, my unknown friend, that a Roslyn will know how to recompense those who have saved his honour.'

With these words the Earl fell back on his lowly pallet, while the stranger hastened to regain the upper earth which he had quitted to fulfil his benevolent errand.

## 8

The old Hall of Military Justice (it has lately been pulled down and a new one erected in its stead) was a vast and gloomy building, surrounded by galleries, and surmounted by a huge dark dome upheld by massive columns, the shadow of whose ponderous shafts, united with the louring roof, diffused around an air of profound and appropriate solemnity.

Here on 25th September 1814, upward of ten thousand people were assembled to view the trial of the Earl of St Clair for high treason. The Duke of Wellington occupied the principal seat among the judges, who were twelve in number. A degree of intense interest contracted every brow as the noble prisoner, loaded with irons and attired in the striking costume of his clan, was led by a guard of soldiers into the centre of the hall. None could behold his lofty bearing, his majestic form, his youthful and handsome features, and the stately gait with which he moved, in spite of his heavy fetters, without experiencing an involuntary conviction that he who stood before them was no traitor.

The first step taken by the Court was to demand a recapitulation of the evidence which had already been adduced. This was accordingly gone into: the jewels, the amulet, the cloth and the sword were all sedulously displayed, and it appeared that nothing was wanting to prove the prisoner's guilt in the most satisfactory manner. 'He is lost beyond redemption,' was the general feeling which pervaded the bosom of every spectator. The Earl was now called upon for his defence. Slowly he rose and with a calm dignity of manner, proceeded to assert his innocence and deprecate the clemency of his judges.

'My lords,' said he, rising in energy as he went on, 'I do not implore an acquittal. That would be the part of a man who, conscious of guilt, seeks mercy as a boon. No, I claim it – it is my right. I am innocent and I demand to be treated as such. I conjure you to do your duty, believe the word of a nobleman whose honour, till now, was never doubted, and reject that of a – what shall I call him? – of a man who, to speak in mild terms, is well known utterly to disregard both truth and honour when injuries, either real or supposed, awake in his bosom the bloodthirsty passion of revenge. And, my lords, for the other witness,' – here he turned his full dark eyes on the perjured page, who shrank as if blighted by his glance – 'I know not what demon has possessed my vassal's breast, what hell-born eloquence has persuaded the orphan who, since his birth, has existed only on my bounty, to aid in the destruction of his lord and benefactor. But this I know: they who shall condemn me for such cursed testimony will sin hath in the eyes of men and angels. My lords, avoid the sin for the sake of that Justice whose servants you profess to be, and whose image stands there the guardian of your hall.' Every eye turned as he spoke to the colossal statue of Justice which stood conspicuous in the light of the lofty window. Meantime the Earl continued: 'My lords, avoid it for your own sake, for I warn you the last St Clair will not die unavenged. There are on the heights of my own Elimbos ten thousand unconquered warriors, seven times that number, fierce as lions and free as eagles, that furnish their crests, dwell in the bosoms of those hundred glens that, ruled by no sovereign, controlled by no laws, lie among the wild Branni hills. And when the news that I am dead, that the house of their chief is fallen, that his name and fame are blasted, shall reach these wild sons of the mist, let my murderers, who cut me off with the sword and under the mask of Justice, tremble in their high places. My lords,

I will say no more. Do as you list and gather the fruit of your deed.'

The question was now put whether he had any witnesses to call. For a moment he was silent and seemed lost in deep thought but, almost immediately, raising his head, he said in a firm tone, 'I believe there is one in this hall who if he can will do me great service.'

There was a pause. The judges (except the Duke who throughout the trial had preserved his usual imperturbable calmness of demeanour) regarded each other with looks of astonishment. The exulting smile which had begun to dawn on Colonel Percy's cheek vanished, the page turned pale, and St Clair's own countenance assumed an expression of anxious expectation. At length a slight bustle was heard in one part of the hall, a movement became perceivable among the dense and hitherto almost motionless mass of spectators, their close ranks slowly opened, and a young man of handsome and genteel appearance, attired in an officer's undress uniform, advanced to the judges' seats.

'Are you come to bear testimony in favour of the prisoner?' asked the Duke of Wellington.

'I am,' replied the young officer, bowing respectfully to his interrogator.

'What is your name and your profession?'

'My name is John Bud, and I hold the rank of Ensign in the sixty-fifth regiment of horse, commanded by Colonel Percy.'

'Repeat what you know concerning this affair. But first let the oath be administered to him.'

This formula being complied with, Ensign Bud proceeded to give evidence to the following effect: that on the night preceding that on which the army received orders to attack the enemy's camp, he was returning to his own tent after passing the evening with a friend, when just as he passed the outskirts of a thick grove of trees beside the river, the words: 'Thou shalt obey me this instant, dwarf, or I'll stab thee to the heart' caught his ear; that on looking through the branches he beheld Colonel Percy and a man dressed in livery holding between them a little boy whom he believed to be the same now present in Their Lordships' Court; that the child fell on his knees and promised to obey them in everything; that the colonel then told him to go to the African camp and claim a reward in the name of his master, the Earl of St Clair, for intelligence of an important nature concerning certain plans which had just been resolved on in a council of war; that on the boy's declaring that he did not know the way, the colonel said he would go with him as far as the boundaries; that then, after wrapping himself in a green plaid which he took from the child, all three left the place and were soon out of sight. As the witness concluded this singular piece of evidence, Colonel Percy started from his seat and sprung rather than stepped to the bar.

'My lords,' he exclaimed, in a loud but agitated voice, which, while his flushed cheek, fierce eye, and the veins swelled almost to bursting on his forehead, proclaimed the violence of the emotions that were contending within him. 'My lords, I implore you not to believe a word which has been uttered by that forsworn, that perjured minion. Mean revenge has dictated –'

He was going on with increasing vehemence when the Duke of Wellington commanded silence. A short conference carried on in such low tones as scarcely to be audible then succeeded among the judges, the result of which was that they declared that Ensign Bud's testimony was not sufficiently clear and decisive to warrant an immediate acquittal, but that they should remand the prisoner for the present in order that he might have an opportunity of procuring further evidence. The court was now about to dissolve when a movement became again visible among the crowd. It opened a second time, and our friend, Mr S'death, appeared, followed by six men, bearing a litter on which lay a man dressed in the blue silver-laced coat of a footman. His countenance was ghastly pale and his clothes were covered with recent stains of blood. 'Set him down here at the foot of his master as in duty bound,' said Mr S'death, coming forward with an air of bustling assiduity, and carefully assisting the men to deposit their doleful burden just beside Colonel Percy.

'What do you mean by this, you villain?' asked he, turning as pale as the dying man before him.

S'death answered this question by a quiet inward chuckle and a significant nod of intelligence. Then, turning to the Duke, he said, 'You see, my lord, I was daunering out this morning up the valley to get a breath of country air when, just as I got to a very lonely and quiet spot, I heard a long rattling groan, like as it might be of a man that's either drunk or discontented. So I turned to the place it seemed to come from and what should I see but this here carrion lying writhing on the ground like a trodden snake. "What's to do with you?" says I, "and who's brought you to that smart pass, my beauty?" "Colonel Percy," he squealed out. "Oh carry me to Verdopolis, carry me to the Hall of Justice! Let me be revenged on the wretch before I die!" There was no resisting this pathetic appeal. Besides, I have a great affection for the colonel and knowing him to be a wildish young man – youth alas! has its follies as well as old age – I thought the sight of his poor servant in the death throes might do him good, so I ran, hired a litter and brought him here according to his wish.'

'What is the meaning of all this?' asked the Duke. 'Who is the wounded man?'

'I am a miserable and deluded being,' replied Travers, in a hollow, tremulous tone, 'but if it please Heaven to grant me strength and time for confession, I will ease my conscience of a part at least of that fiery burden which presses on it. Let it be known to all in this place that the Earl of St Clair is totally innocent of the crime laid to his charge. My master is the traitor. Yes – but – but I cannot get on…' Here he paused from exhaustion, his eyes closed, his breath came thick, and to all present it appeared as if he was dying. On a glass of wine being administered to him, however, he revived in some degree. Raising himself on his litter, he requested to speak with St Clair in private. Orders were immediately given for the crowd to be cleared out. The subordinate judges likewise removed to a distant part of the hall, and none remained within hearing of his confession except the Duke of Wellington, Ensign Bud, and the Earl himself. This being done, the poor wretch proceeded thus.

'My lord, Colonel Percy hates you for what reasons you yourself best know. He recognised you for an old enemy at the Olympic Games, and ordered me after the prizes were distributed to watch your motions and inform him where you should take up quarters for the night. I dogged you as far as the Zephyr Valley, and then returned to tell my master. When we returned you were fast asleep, and that boy, whom from his dress, short stature and withered unnatural features, my master always called the green dwarf, was laid at your feet. The colonel then bade me go and fetch the boy to him. I did so, and when he was brought, Percy drew his sword and threatened to kill him on the spot if he would not instantly swear to obey him in everything he should command. The lad called out that if he did obey him it should be for the promise of a reward rather than for a threat of punishment. My master told him to name his own reward; he said he would do so when he knew what his business was to be. Colonel Percy told him in the first place it was to tell him who his master was. He said he would do that for five pounds, and then confessed directly that you were the Earl of St Clair. Afterwards the colonel told him he was to be a spy on all your actions, to note particularly whether you went to Clydesdale Castle, to follow you thither, if possible to listen at the door of the apartment to which you might be shown, and to report everything that was said to him. The little mercenary wretch swore to do all this for a hundred pounds. He was then informed in what part of the city his employer resided, and dismissed to commence his villainous system of espial. About a week afterwards he arrived at our house panting and quite out of breath, and desired to see the colonel instantly. He had brought information that you and Lady Emily Charlesworth had concerted a plan of elopement together which was to be put in practice at twelve o'clock that night. My master commanded him to delay you as much beyond the time as he could, and then dismissed him. At eleven o'clock, he and myself set off in a carriage and six for the castle. We reached the place of rendezvous – a chestnut avenue – shortly after twelve. At the entrance my master got out and went a little way up the walk; he soon returned with the lady and handed her into the carriage.

'Did she go with him willingly?' asked St Clair, in a tone of the deepest agitation.

'Yes, but it was because he had passed himself for you, and as he had on a travelling cloak, and the trees threw a very dark shade, it was impossible for her to discover the cheat.'

'But she might have recognised his voice – he spoke to her, did he not?'

'Very seldom, and when he did it was scarcely above his breath.'

'Well, proceed: where did you carry her?'

'That I cannot, dare not tell. I am bound by a solemn oath never to reveal it, and surely you would not have me add fresh agonies to my dying hour by committing the crime of perjury?'

In this determination the man seemed fixed. St Clair tried in vain arguments, entreaties and commands, and seeing it was impossible to prevail with him, and that the sands of life were running very low, he at length permitted him to continue his confession.

'When she was secured,' said he, 'we returned to Verdopolis, and the next day accompanied the rest of the army on their march against the rebels. You arrived at the camp shortly after us. As soon as he saw you, my master resolved to rid himself of an abhorred rival in your person, and was confirmed in this resolution by seeing the distinction with which His Grace the Duke of Wellington treated you. Accordingly, one night he ordered me to fetch him the green dwarf. I proceeded to your tent for this purpose and, by means of a peculiar signal with which he was acquainted, called him out. Subsequently, by means of threats and promises, the dwarf was induced to lend his aid in executing the scheme which my master had devised for your disgrace and death. He went to the camp, betrayed the secrets of the council in your name, and brought back as recompense the articles which are now lying on that table. These he afterwards buried in your tent. He removed the sword which was fastened to your belt, and put that scimitar in its place, and finally he completed his treachery by delivering that false evidence which has so nearly been the means of causing you to incur an undeserved and shameful death.'

Here Travers paused again to wipe off the death-sweats which were starting in large drops from his pallid forehead.

'You have nobly cleared St Clair's character,' said the Duke of Wellington. 'Now inform us by whom and how the wound of which you are dying has been afflicted.'

'By my master,' replied the unhappy man. 'I informed him this morning as we were returning from his uncle's country seat in the valley that I intended to reform and lead a better life, for that the sins I had already committed lay like a leaden weight at my heart. At first he laughed at me and pretended to think I was in jest, but on my assuring him that I never was more serious in my life, he grew gloomy. We walked together for some time in silence, but at length, just as we came to a very lonely part of the road, he drew his sword and stabbed me suddenly in the side, saying, as I fell, with a loud laugh, "Now go and reform in hell!" I can speak no longer and you know the rest.'

The last part of Travers' communication was uttered in a very faint and broken voice. When the excitement of talking was past, he fell into a sort of lethargy which continued about ten minutes and then, with a single gasping groan and convulsive shudder of the whole frame, his soul and body parted for ever asunder.

The crowd were now again admitted into the hall. The judges returned to their station, and the Duke of Wellington, after publicly declaring that St Clair's honour was unblemished and that the charge brought against him had risen entirely from the machinations of a malignant enemy, ordered his fetters to be taken off and commanded them to be fastened on the limbs of Colonel Percy and the green dwarf instead. Subsequently he condemned the former of these worthy personages to death, and the latter to ten years' labour at the galleys.

Matters being thus settled, the Duke rose from his seat and, taking St Clair by the hand, he said, 'My lord, I claim you as my guest while you remain in Verdopolis. You must comply with my request were it only to show that you bear no malice against me for the six weeks' imprisonment to which you have been subjected.'

Of course St Clair could not resist such an invitation thus courteously urged, and accordingly he accompanied the Duke to Waterloo Palace. On his way thither he informed his noble conductor of the mysterious incognito who had visited him in his dungeon, and expressed a strong desire to discover who he was that he might recompense him according to the signal service he had received at his hands.

'Was it Ensign Bud, do you think?' said the Duke.

'No,' replied St Clair. 'He was taller, and the tones of his voice were very different. Indeed, if I may be permitted to form so presumptuous a conjecture on such slight grounds, I should say that I am at this moment conversing with my unknown friend.'

The Duke smiled but returned no answer.

'I am not mistaken then,' continued St Clair easily, 'and it is to Your Grace that I owe a continuance both of life and honour.'

As he spoke, the silent gratitude which beamed forth from his fine eyes expressed his thanks more clearly than any words could have done.

'Well,' said the Duke, 'I will confess that you have made a true guess, and now I suppose you would like to know the reasons which led me in the first place to give you that warning on the banks of the Senegal. It was simply this. I had witnessed the sort of quarrel which took place between you and Colonel Percy during supper in my pavilion. I saw him lay his hand on his sword and then relinquish it with a look and a muttered exclamation which told me plainly that the gratification of present revenge was postponed only for some more delicious future prospect, and as the life of the chieftain of Clan Albyn was of some value in my estimation, I determined at least to set him on his guard against the attempts of an insidious enemy. Then for my visit in the prison: that was prompted by the information Ensign Bud had communicated to me, and I thought that that method of summoning him to give evidence which I pointed out would make a deeper impression on the minds of the other judges than if the ordinary way of calling a witness was followed.'

As the Duke concluded this explanation they reached Waterloo Palace. They immediately proceeded to the dining-room where dinner was already prepared. During this meal St Clair spoke very little and ate less. His spirits, which had been in some degree excited by the unexpected events of the morning, now began to flag. The thought of Lady Emily, and of the forlorn and wretched condition to which she was probably reduced, communicated a mournful gloom to his mind. The Duke perceived this, and after a few vain attempts to dispel it, he said, 'I see what you are thinking of, my lord, so come, I'll carry you to my wife. Perhaps her sympathy will be some consolation to your distress.'

St Clair followed almost mechanically as his noble host led the way to the drawing-room. On entering, they found the Duchess seated on the sofa and engaged in some ornamental labour of the needle. Beside her was a little Indian stand supporting her work-box and a few books. Near this, and with her back turned to the door, was seated another elegant female form, over whose rich brown tresses was thrown a transparent veil of white gauze, according to the graceful fashion of the times. Her head was resting on her hand in a pensive posture, and when the Duke and his guest were announced, she did not rise nor give any other symptom of being conscious of their presence, except a sudden and convulsive start. The Duchess, however, left her seat and advanced to meet St Clair with a benignant smile.

'I was sure,' said she, 'that justice would be done and that your fame would come out of the fiery ordeal seven times purified.[24] Now, my lord, will you permit me to introduce you to a friend of mine. Here, love' – addressing the silent lady – 'is one whom Fortune has severely tried, and now expects from her and you a recompense for all he has suffered.'

The lady rose, threw back her veil, there was a momentary pause, a joyful exclamation, and St Clair clasped to his bosom his dear and long-lost Emily.

It now only remains for me to explain how this happy catastrophe was brought about, which duty I shall discharge as briefly as possible.

During a period of four weeks, Lady Emily had pined in her lonely prison under the surveillance of the wretched Bertha, who regularly visited her three times a day to supply her with food, but at all other times remained in a distant part of the castle. At the usual hour on the first day of the fifth week, she did not make her appearance. Lady Emily, whose appetite was much impaired by grief and confinement, at first was rather pleased than otherwise with the omission. But when night came, she began to feel some symptoms of hunger. The next day likewise elapsed, and neither food nor drink passed her now parched and quivering lips. On the morning of the third day, she was reduced to such a state of weakness from inanition that she felt totally unable to leave her bed.

While she lay there expecting death and almost wishing for it, the tramp of a heavy step in the antechamber and the sound of a gruff voice calling out, 'Is there any living body besides owls and bats in this here old ancient heap of a ruin?' roused her from the lethargic stupor into which she had fallen. Collecting her remaining strength with a strong effort, she answered that there was an unhappy woman imprisoned here who would give much for deliverance and a restoration to her friends.

Apparently the querist heard her voice, faint as it was, for he immediately broke open the door of her chamber and appeared in the shape of a tall and athletic man, dressed in the usual garb of rare lads and armed with a long fowling piece. 'What's to do with you, poor heart, that you look so pale and thin?' said he, advancing towards her. She shortly informed him that she had eaten nothing for three days, and begged a little food for the love of heaven. He directly took from a pouch, which was slung over his shoulder, a little bread and cheese. While she was eating these coarse though acceptable viands, he told her that his name was Dick Crackskull, and that while poaching a bit in the forest, he had lit upon this old tower which, from motives of idle curiosity, he had entered through one of the unglazed windows; that in his per-ambulations through the desolate halls he had, to his horror, stumbled on the corpse of an old and hideous woman who, to his mind, looked for all the world like a witch; that he then supposed that there must be some other inhabitants, and so had gone bawling as he went on, till he reached the antechamber of Lady Emily's apartment, whose life he had thus been the providential means of saving.

The next day, after covering Bertha's dead body with a heap of stones, Dick set out with his charge for Verdopolis. On arriving there he accompanied the lady, at her own desire, to Waterloo Palace. Here she put herself under the Duchess' protection who, after bestowing on Dick a reward that made his heart leap for joy, dismissed him with all honour.

From my mother the unfortunate damsel received the most tender and assiduous kindness insomuch that she won her entire confidence, and all the tale of Lady Emily's mournful loves was poured into her beloved patroness' sympathising ear. When the news of Lord St Clair's incarceration for high treason arrived, her grief may be better imagined than described. But now the pleasure of this happy meeting, when she received her lover with life untouched and honour unsullied, more than counterbalanced all her past tears and agony. The good old Marquis of Charlesworth was now easily brought to consent to their union and, according to all accounts, never was felicity so lasting and unbroken as that which crowned the future lives of the noble Earl of St Clair and the beautiful Lady Emily Charlesworth.

Having thus wound up the denouement of my brief and jejune narrative, I will conclude by a glance at the future fortunes of Colonel Percy and his accomplices.

The sentence of death which had been passed on the former was afterwards commuted to exile for sixteen years. During this period he wandered through the world, sometimes a pirate, sometimes the leader of banditti, and ever the companion of the most dissolute and profligate of mankind. At the expiration of the term of banishment, he returned to Verdopolis, broken both in health and fortune, to claim the inheritance of his uncle, the Duke of Beaufort, who had been for some time dead. On enquiry, however, he found that the nobleman had married shortly after his disgrace became known, and had become the father of two sons, on whom, consequently, his estates and title devolved. Thus baffled, the colonel turned his attention to political affairs, and finding himself disowned by all his relations, discarded his real name and assumed a feigned one. Few now can recognise in that seditious demagogue, that worn-out and faded debauchee Alexander Rogue, Viscount Ellrington, the once brilliant and handsome soldier Colonel Augustus Percy.[25]

As for Andrew, when he was released from his service on the galleys, he became a printer's devil; from thence he rose to the office of compositor, and being of a saving and pilfering disposition, he at length by some means acquired money enough to purchase a commission in the army. He then took to the trade of author, published drivelling rhymes which he called Poetry, and snivelling tales which went under the denomination of novels.

I need say no more. Many are yet living who can discover a passage in the early life of Captain Tree in this my tale of the green dwarf.

# NOTES

1. Brontë is here referring to the group of literary women who met together in London in the 1750s and who were decried as The Blue Stockings Society, supposedly for their unfashionable choice of attire.

2. Verdopolis is Greek for 'glass town', the name the Brontës adopted for the setting of much of their juvenilia.

3. Calenture is a tropical disease whose symptoms include delirium. Sailors suffering from it were reputed to have jumped overboard to their deaths in the belief that the sea was in fact green fields.

4. Restored a little.

5. Captain Tree and his son, Sergeant Tree, appear in much of the Brontës' juvenilia. Captain Tree was also an early pseudonym of Charlotte Brontë.

6. A Spanish wine.

7. Charles Wellesley was Charlotte Brontë's preferred pseudonym throughout her juvenilia.

8. The four Chief Genii, Tali, Brani, Emi and Anni, were Charlotte, Branwell, Emily and Anne Brontë respectively.

9. This is in fact a description of a set of wooden soldiers once owned by the Brontë children.

10. A sweet Spanish wine.

11. Gifford has been thought to represent Branwell Brontë; the dialogue here is then a satire on Branwell's penchant for introducing antiquarian learning into his early writing.

12. Melchizedek, priest and King of Salem, blessed Abraham by giving him bread and wine, and in return Abraham granted him a tenth of all he possessed. (Genesis 14: 18–20)

13. It was a tradition among the Brontë children that, thousands of years earlier, twelve 'giants' from Britain had travelled to Africa and to the land of the Genii.

14. The ensuing tale (from here until the end of Chapter 1) was published separately in the 1925 collection *The Twelve Adventurers and Other Stories* under the title 'Napoleon and the Spectre'.

15. The poor little storyteller.

16. The African Olympic Games was a recurring event in the Brontës' juvenilia, probably inspired by accounts of the ancient Greek games, and by the fiction of Sir Walter Scott (1772–1832), in particular *Ivanhoe* (1819).

17. Nebuchadnezzar issued a decree ordering all his officials to assemble on the plain of Dura in Babylon to worship the golden statue he had erected. (Daniel 3: 1–3)

18. The old gentleman is of course the devil.

19. The Twelves were a set of toy soldiers, belonging to Branwell, which inspired many of the Brontës' stories.

20. This is not strictly consistent, Lady Emily Charlesworth having been introduced as the niece of Bravey at the African Olympic Games.

21. *Il Penseroso* and *L'Allegro* are both poems by John Milton (1608–74), *Il Penseroso* (1632) being addressed to the Goddess of Melancholy, and *L'Allegro* (1632) to the Goddess of Mirth.

22. Little song.

23. A hempen neckcloth is the noose used in hangings.

24. A reference to the fiery furnace into which Shadrach, Meshach and Abednego were cast for refusing to bow down and worship the golden statue, and from which they emerged unscathed. (Daniel 3)

25. The description of Colonel Percy's later life is based on Branwell Brontë's *The Pirate* (1833) and *Real Life on Verdopolis* (1833).

# BIOGRAPHICAL NOTE

Charlotte Brontë was born in Thornton, Yorkshire, in 1816. In 1820 her father was appointed curate at Haworth and the family moved to Haworth Parsonage where Charlotte was to spend most of her life. Following the death of her mother in 1821 and of her two eldest sisters in 1825, she and her two surviving sisters, Emily and Anne, and brother, Branwell, were brought up by their father and a devoutly religious aunt.

Theirs was an unhappy childhood, in particular the period the sisters spent at a school for daughters of the clergy. Charlotte abhorred the harsh regime, blaming it for the deaths of her two sisters, and she went on to fictionalise her experiences there in *Jane Eyre* (1847). Having been removed from the school, the three sisters, together with Branwell, found solace in storytelling. Inspired by a set of toy soldiers, they created the imaginary kingdoms of Angria and Gondal which form the settings for much of their juvenilia. From 1831 to 1832 Charlotte was educated at Roe Head school where she later returned as a teacher.

In 1842 Charlotte travelled to Brussels with Emily. They returned home briefly following the death of their aunt, but, soon after, Charlotte was back in Brussels, this time as a teacher. At great expense, the three sisters published a volume of poetry – *Poems by Currer, Ellis and Acton Bell* (1846) – but this proved unsuccessful, selling only two copies. By the time of its publication, each of the sisters had completed a novel: Emily's *Wuthering Heights* and Anne's *Agnes Grey* were both published in 1848, but Charlotte's novel, *The Professor*, remained unpublished in her lifetime. Undeterred, Charlotte embarked on *Jane Eyre* which was published in 1847 and hailed by Thackeray as 'the masterwork of a great genius'. She followed this up with *Shirley* (1849) and *Villette* (1853), and continued to be published under the pseudonym Currer Bell although her identity was, by now, well known.

Branwell, in many ways the least successful of the four siblings, died in 1848. His death deeply distressed the sisters, and both Emily and Anne died within the following year. Charlotte married her father's curate in 1854, but she died in the early stages of pregnancy in March 1855.

## HESPERUS PRESS – 100 PAGES

Hesperus Press, as suggested by the Latin motto, is committed to bringing near what is far – far both in space and time. Works written by the greatest authors, and unjustly neglected or simply little known in the English-speaking world, are made accessible through new translations and a completely fresh editorial approach. Through these short classic works, each around 100 pages in length, the reader will be introduced to the greatest writers from all times and all cultures.

For more information on Hesperus Press, please visit our website: **www.hesperuspress.com**

ET REMOTISSIMA PROPE

## SELECTED TITLES FROM HESPERUS PRESS

Gustave Flaubert *Memoirs of a Madman*

Alexander Pope *Scriblerus*

Ugo Foscolo *Last Letters of Jacopo Ortis*

Anton Chekhov *The Story of a Nobody*

Joseph von Eichendorff *Life of a Good-for-nothing*

MarkTwain *The Diary of Adam and Eve*

Giovanni Boccaccio *Life of Dante*

Victor Hugo *The Last Day of a Condemned Man*

Joseph Conrad *Heart of Darkness*

Edgar Allan Poe *Eureka*

Emile Zola *For a Night of Love*

Daniel Defoe *The King of Pirates*

Giacomo Leopardi *Thoughts*

Nikolai Gogol *The Squabble*

Franz Kafka *Metamorphosis*

Herman Melville *The Enchanted Isles*

Leonardo daVinci *Prophecies*

Charles Baudelaire *On Wine and Hashish*

William MakepeaceThackeray *Rebecca and Rowena*

Wilkie Collins *Who Killed Zebedee?*

Théophile Gautier *The Jinx*

Charles Dickens *The Haunted House*

Luigi Pirandello *Loveless Love*

Fyodor Dostoevsky *Poor People*

E.T.A. Hoffmann *Mademoiselle de Scudéri*

Henry James *In the Cage*

Francis Petrarch *My Secret Book*

André Gide *Theseus*

D.H. Lawrence *The Fox*

Percy Bysshe Shelley *Zastrozzi*

Marquis de Sade *Incest*

Oscar Wilde *The Portrait of Mr W.H.*

Giacomo Casanova *The Duel*

LeoTolstoy *Hadji Murat*

Friedrich von Schiller *The Ghost-seer*

Nathaniel Hawthorne *Rappaccini's Daughter*

Pietro Aretino *The School of Whoredom*

Honoré de Balzac *Colonel Chabert*

Thomas Hardy *Fellow-Townsmen*

Arthur Conan Doyle *The Tragedy of the Korosko*

Stendhal *Memoirs of an Egotist*

Katherine Mansfield *In a German Pension*

Giovanni Verga *Life in the Country*

IvanTurgenev *Faust*

Theodor Storm *The Lake of the Bees*

F. Scott Fitzgerald *The Rich Boy*

Dante Alighieri *New Life*

Guy de Maupassant *Butterball*

Elizabeth Gaskell *Lois the Witch*

Joris-Karl Huysmans *With the Flow*

George Eliot *Amos Barton*

Gabriele D'Annunzio *The Book of the Virgins*

Heinrich von Kleist *The Marquise of O–*

Alexander Pushkin *Dubrovsky*